THE WOMEN WARRIORS

Before long, shadowy shapes began appearing over the ridge, coming into the torchlight. First of all came Two Big Feet, stripped to a loincloth and carrying a club. Her dark skin shone with grease in the reddish glare. Before Two Big Feet came stamping into the circle of light, Second Son bent for a rock and let fly at the woman's head, knocking her flat. In a moment the club was in Second Son's hand, and she sent it zinging into the darkness.

Then she backed away and gestured for her opponent to rise. Shaking her head, Two Big Feet pushed herself up. She looked a bit dazed, and a thin trickle of blood ran down her face from the spot where the rock had struck her.

Second Son sprang like a puma, tucked together, her entire weight landing solidly at the level of the woman's shoulders. Unbalanced, the Ute went down again with Second Son on top of her. Then, sitting on her back, Second Son pounded her head onto the gritty soil of the mountain until she lay still, not even trying to push herself up again. Two Big Feet groaned, and the Cheyenne allowed her to lift her head a bit.

There was a gasp from the watching women as they saw the bruised and bloody face of their leader. Then Second Son looked up at Standing Bird, wife of the Pawnee. "Hand me your knife," she said, and her tone brooked no disobedience.

The woman drew her skinning knife from its sling at her waist and held it hesitantly toward Second Son, her expression terrified. The warrior put her foot on the chest of the gasping Ute and reached for her wild tangle of hair. . . .

MOUNTAIN MAJESTY

ASK YOUR BOOKSELLER
FOR THE BOOKS YOU HAVE MISSED

Book One: *WILD COUNTRY*
Book Two: *THE UNTAMED*
Book Three: *WILDERNESS RENDEZVOUS*
Book Four: *BLOOD KIN*
Book Five: *PASSAGE WEST*

Mountain Majesty

BOOK FIVE

PASSAGE WEST

JOHN KILLDEER

BANTAM BOOKS
NEW YORK • TORONTO • LONDON • SYDNEY • AUCKLAND

PASSAGE WEST

A Bantam Domain Book / January 1994

ISBN 0-553-56376-9

Published simultaneously in the United States and Canada

Bantam Books are published by Bantam Books, a division of Bantam Doubleday Dell Publishing Group, Inc. Its trademark, consisting of the words "Bantam Books" and the portrayal of a rooster, is Registered in U.S. Patent and Trademark Office and in other countries. Marca Registrada. Bantam Books, 1540 Broadway, New York, New York 10036.

PRINTED IN THE UNITED STATES OF AMERICA

RAD 0 9 8 7 6 5 4 3 2 1

making their way toward the summer Rendezvous on the Green River, Cleve had talked about Ferris and their long friendship. They had shared adventures and dangers over the years, and he hoped to see the old codger again.

Much to Cleve's delight, he and his wife, Second Son, had found the old trapper's small cabin still sitting solidly under the shelter of a huge fir tree, smoke curling from its pole-and-cat chimney. Around it the tender green of a mountain spring lighted the countryside.

Cleve was surprised at the depth of his relief. When the pack train, laden with furs, halted at the edge of the clearing and Cleve gave the whistle that had always been their private signal, the old fellow had stepped out of the thicket of young firs beside the house, rifle in hand.

He was still alert as ever, Cleve thought, although it had been years since he had set a trap or skinned out a beaver plew. Hunting had always been his favorite pastime, and evidently it kept him fit and fed.

Now, filled with a stew of rabbit and duck and venison and just about every other sort of game you could think of, Cleve basked beside the fire as they caught their friend up with the news, some of which was several years old.

"William Ashworth did sell out his fur-trading business," he told Ferris. "I hear he's gone into politics back in Missouri. He's one smart man—got out for a fair price before the trapping got so poor. We worked our butts off this past winter, and four bales is all we've come out with."

"I seen it comin', way back when the young'un there was just a tad," Ferris said, emitting a long puff of tobacco smoke. "Trappin's only as good as the beaver, besides bein' a young man's game, not for some old bastard with rheumatiz in the joints that makes his hands hell for handlin' cold, dead carcasses and freezin' traps." Ferris spat into the fire.

"I figured it was just as well, me being a preacher, that I didn't go nigh any more of them Rendezvous, too. Too much hellin' and whorin' for my taste, and nothing I could say made a dime's worth of difference. You turn young men loose with whiskey and red-tail wenches—beggin' your pardon, Second Son—and there's just no tellin' what will happen. All of it bad, o' course."

Second Son's smile was only a slight widening of her lips, but Cleve knew she was remembering their first Rendezvous when this woman-hating preacher had saved her from a bunch of drunken trappers bent on raping her. She'd had a soft spot in her heart for him ever since. Billy-Wolf, then an infant, had been strapped to her back, and both of them might well have died if he hadn't lent a hand.

The boy had crept around the hearth to sit beside Ferris's knee. His dark eyes were wide and bright, and he kept patting Ferris as if he could hardly believe he was actually there. "Did you know we went to see Dad's kin back in Missouri?" he asked in English. "And I got shot!"

He pulled back his leather shirt and proudly showed the scar, now only a pale streak on the underside of his arm. He never tired of bragging about it. Few young ones boasted such a thing, at his age, and he had got a lot of mileage out of it back in the Burning Heart village, when they visited his mother's Cheyenne kin.

"That's a right smart scar you got there," Ferris said, leaning forward and touching the reddish line to give it its due. "Your pa told me about them fellows, and I take it they lived to rue the day."

Billy-Wolf nodded, though his father knew he hadn't a clue as to the meaning of the words *rue the day*. "My brother Rakes the Sky with Lightning says this is the mark of a warrior," he said.

Ferris looked across at Cleve and raised one grizzled eyebrow. Cleve sighed. "Big heads come in all sizes," he said. "My ma wouldn't know him now—he's not only grown a foot in height, but he's got all bold and sassy, to boot."

Abashed, Billy-Wolf settled back to sit between the dogs. Snip and Jase were quiet, alert, but here in the shelter of Ferris's house, they came as near to relaxing as they ever could.

Cleve knew that any untoward sound outside would bring four ears up, four brown eyes turning toward whatever it was, and an almost inaudible growl of warning to two canine throats. Having dogs trained to watch and guard was valuable in this still-untamed country.

Second Son came to sit beside Cleve and busied her hands with fletching new arrows, though she already had enough completed for all of them. The woman could not sit still, that was the problem. All her life she had been doing something, and in that, he realized, she was much like her white counterparts.

Except that Second Son was not only a wife and a mother, she was also a warrior, a hunter, a trapper, and a guide of superb skill. To her own people she was a man, which had been known to make his relationship with her awkward at times.

It had been many years since any newcomer to the Rendezvous had dared to raise a hand against her. The first time she had been faced fairly, instead of being ambushed as those drunken men had done at their first Rendezvous, the challenger had been soundly beaten by a combination of strength and unexpected tricks worthy of a fox.

The second time she was attacked, the man barely escaped with his life. Cleve himself had asked her to spare him so they would not fall under the strict rule against killing within the confines of the Rendezvous. Only because of that had she let Julio Cardenas Morales live.

Thinking about the man still gave Cleve a chill between his shoulder blades. The Mexican was a dangerous man. He had heard the tales of the other trappers gathered there, three years before. Then the fool had made a point of confronting Second Son and insulting her both as a Cheyenne and as a woman.

If he'd said to Cleve something as inflammatory as he'd said to Second Son, Cleve might not have been able to stop himself from killing the Mexican. It told a lot about the control built into his warrior-wife that she had done so.

"Whereabouts be the Rendezvous, this year?" Ferris asked, after a time of companionable silence. "Up to Pierre's Hole agin or over on Green River?"

"Green River," Cleve said. "Not too far a step from here, if you want to go with us and catch up on all the news."

"I get more than I want settin' right here to home," Ferris said. "Asa Ketcham was by last fall griping about how skeerce the beaver are gettin'. With all the folks tramplin' through the woods and over the mountains, that's no surprise. The little critters can only raise so many kits in a season, and when you've got numbskulls trappin' 'em before they're old enough to breed, it stands to reason they're goin' to thin out."

"That's no lie," Cleve said, remembering the quickly diminishing number of new beaver lodges. "We trapped in the Swans this season, country we thought hadn't so far been thick with men on the ground, but somebody had been there before us.

"Takings were skimpy. Not that we're hurting for cash—Second Son won't let me spend it helling around, so it stacks up. Still, we're thinking about going back to our old original stomping ground in the Absarokas."

"Your secret valley you told me about? That might be a good idea—if nobody has up and found it, o' course." Ferris pulled thoughtfully at his pipe and watched Cleve through the curl of smoke.

Cleve felt a cold lump in the pit of his stomach. Somehow it had never occurred to him that anyone else but he and Second Son and Billy-Wolf would ever set foot in that steep-walled valley below the waterfall. The idea made him feel slightly sick.

Ferris leaned to push a fresh chunk of wood onto the fire. "Too many white men here now," he complained. "Injuns, now, they move through the country and you can't hardly tell where they've been. Our kind is different. We seem like we got to leave our mark, be it good or bad."

Cleve thought of the stink of Rendezvous, wherever it might be held. Only those who got there early breathed air untainted by shit and smoke and dirty human hide.

Ferris reloaded his pipe, which he had taken to smoking after he retired from trapping. Any visitor intending to stop by his cabin brought a gift of tobacco, and Cleve had held on to a packet for two years, hoping to find his way past Old Joe's house. Now he grinned as the smoke again began to curl about the old man's head.

"You old goat, you ought to go with us anyway. There's lots of men would be might happy to see your ugly mug again," he said.

"You would be welcome to stay in our lodge," Second Son added, looking up from her arrows.

"And we could play together every day," Billy-Wolf said. He seemed to think of Ferris as a rather overgrown child, for the two of them sometimes rampaged ridiculously, on the occasions when they had the chance.

"I'll think on it," the preacher said. He blew a smoke ring, which never failed to fascinate the boy. "It has been a while, at that. Old Emile—he's still alive and kicking, I reckon?"

Cleve nodded. "Emile Prévot will go when he and God see fit and not one minute before. Nobody, white or red, has ever outfoxed that one. He still goes down into the lodges, too, and I'm told he's been known to wear out the woman he picks before he goes home in the dawn."

Second Son frowned. She resented the behavior of the people from different tribes who sold their wives for money or trade goods. Among her Cheyenne people, self-restraint was taught from the cradle board, and promiscuousness was not known.

A faithless wife, in fact, was cast out, "a woman on the plain," for the use of anyone who happened to pass. She was never referred to again among her own kind. It was the most terrible of fates for any woman.

"When those who sell their women make men think all red women are of that kind, it makes my life much harder," she said. She thrust another arrow into the bundle and took up the moccasin she had been lacing together. "I must fight for my honor against men who would not attack me if they had not been misled by those animals down in the lodges."

Ferris tapped his pipe against his heel. "Might be I ought to go along this year, just to see to such things. I'd kind of like to jaw awhile with old Emile and Jim Bridwell, too.

"I started to name a few more, but they're all dead now, more's the pity. If I don't go now, who's to say if anybody will be left when I get ready to travel again?"

"Now that's what I wanted to hear!" Cleve said, rising and pulling Second Son up with him. "Tomorrow we'll put your plunder together, and the next day or so we'll take off for Green River, all together like old times."

Billy-Wolf was dancing up and down like a fox kit, his eyes bright in the firelight. His mother put her hand on his shoulder and brought him to a halt.

"We will sleep now," she commanded, and the boy turned at once to his bedroll and spread it before the fire.

"Will we see that man Morales again?" the child asked, after he had curled into the furs necessary even in the spring at such altitudes. He had been old enough to remember that battle between his mother and the Mexican.

Second Son looked up, and Cleve caught her glance. He bent over his son. "Now why would you ask something like that?"

"Because I dreamed about him last night. He was big and mean, but I knew it was that man. Funny thing, though . . ." His voice was already trailing off as sleep overtook the child. "He had a head like a buffalo. A big old mean bull, with shiny frost all over his horns."

Cleve and his wife stared at each other, their eyes widening. Never had they mentioned to their son the bull buffalo that had been Cleve's first totem. They had not spoken of his mother's dream of running from just such a buffalo down a long tunnel, only to find it waiting at the end, staring at her with death in its eyes.

Those dreams had been true medicine dreams, and they had been fulfilled, amid danger and death. But they had been put away with completed matters. Why was their son dreaming of the beast again?

That dream had always foretold danger. The combination of the buffalo and Morales was an ominous one, Cleve felt in his bones.

But they said nothing. Second Son bent over Billy-Wolf and pulled the fur about his shoulders. "Sleep now, my son. Dream of pleasant things—riding on the shoulders of our old friend at Rendezvous or playing with the children who come up from the lodges.

"We are here, your father and I, and you are safe. Remember that."

But when she turned to Cleve, he saw that her face was grim. Her expression echoed his own feeling that this would not be an easy journey.

chapter

—2—

Julio Cardena Morales had spent three winters nursing a grudge that grew with the passing of time. Although his companion, Felipe Boaz, had been careful not to say a word to him about his defeat at the hands of Cleve Bennett's Cheyenne woman, every time the Spaniard looked into Felipe's eyes he had seen that memory someplace behind his carefully noncommittal expression.

This was not a thing that a man of spirit could bear. It must be washed away in blood, and if that meant killing her man and her son, as well as the *puta* herself, then so be it. He had sworn an oath to avenge that disgrace, and as he traveled toward the Rio Verde he felt the heat of his hatred building inside himself. Soon it would burst forth, and when it did, there would be vengeance to cool the spirit and calm the soul.

The fact that his last two winters of trapping had not brought the expected rich harvest did not improve his temper. Indeed, he caught Felipe looking sideways at him, as if dreading some sudden outburst, whenever the trail proved rough or the packhorses tried to stray aside for a nip of spring greenery.

The *estúpido* had been with him for a long while, and he evidently had learned to see when an outbreak of rage was near at hand. It amused Julio, although he disliked having such a dolt able to read his moods.

They had a long way to travel, for he had tried going far south into the ranges where winters were not so cold. The quality of the fur there was less, but he had hoped that he could make that up in quantity.

It had not worked, for it seemed that everywhere there was a beaver stream, industrious trappers were at work before him. The trapping in the Sangre de Cristos had been no improvement.

He had worked much harder than he liked and gained too little for his efforts. He often thought of Jules Terrebonne and his gang of thieves, who let other men do the hard work of trapping and then harvested their bales of hard-won plews.

Avoiding the still-snowy slopes of the mountains, Morales and Felipe dropped into the edge of the plains country, taking the long way around, but knowing it would require less travel time. As they came over a pass and turned back north toward the Green River Rendezvous site, Morales reined in his sorrel gelding and listened intently.

There were men and horses ahead. He could hear the jingle of harnesses, the low murmur of voices. Another group of trappers must be heading toward the great meeting of the year.

Few of the mountain men were his friends, but he had not made many enemies. Morales knew, almost always, when it was safe to harass someone, and only that glaring mistake with the warrior-woman had contributed to his shame.

It was best to be cautious, however, for no one knew what might be found in the wild ranges. Morales signaled to Felipe to bring the packhorses farther up into the trees.

"I will go and see who rides ahead of us," he said. "You wait here with the plews. It would be too bad to lose even the poor few we gathered, no?"

Obediently Felipe took them into a thicket and halted. He was a stout man in a fight, but he needed someone with a better head than his to do his thinking for him. Morales found him very useful when it came to handling heavy bales or dealing with difficult horses. A man who did not think more than enough to survive could be a useful tool . . . and sometimes a deadly weapon, he had discovered.

But now he concentrated upon the travelers ahead. They had paused in their journey, he thought, for the voices grew more distinct as he approached. The jingle of harness and the creak of leather on leather had stopped.

A laugh boomed on the spring air—a familiar laugh with a hint of cruelty to it. Ben Yoder! Morales smiled, thinking how convenient this meeting might become, if things went as he wished them to. There was no greater villain than Yoder, but Morales had always managed to stay on the big man's good side. Strange that he had just been thinking of Yoder's associate, Terrebonne, so recently. This meeting almost had the feel of fate about it.

He cupped his hands about his mouth and sent out a shrill call. "Yoder! Yoder! Morales has come!"

The sounds ahead stopped abruptly. Then there came the sound of plodding hooves, and the big dun that he had traded to Yoder two years before came into view.

The man on his back was a burden even for such a big animal, for there were few among the trapping fraternity who were more massive than Ben Yoder. Or more cruel and devious, Morales knew all too well.

"Julio," Yoder grunted, using the *j* sound instead of the proper Spanish pronunciation. "You comin' in for Rendezvous? I sort of figgered you might've went the other way, off toward the Swans." His sly grin told the Mexican that Yoder, too, knew that the Bennetts had gone in that direction.

"The world, she is trapped out, I think," Morales said. "I try the south, and it is the same there. Only a few skins, and those not so good. And you?"

Yoder grinned, showing brownish-yellow teeth beneath his scruffy mustache. "I always manage to find some good plews," he said. "Somehow or another." He snickered, overly satisfied with his wit.

Morales smiled in turn. He had known for years that Yoder trapped the trappers, when he could. When Jules Terrebonne disappeared, Yoder had taken over the men, the horses, and the ways of that notorious thief and one-time *coureur de bois*. From time to time Morales had given information or other subtle assistance in the man's shady work, and the two of them understood each other well.

"If you agree, we might travel together to the Green," Morales said. "I have only myself and Felipe and four packhorses. It is safer to ride in numbers when you approach the great trade, *sí*?"

Yoder grunted again, this time with agreement. Nobody knew better than he the dangers that might befall a small band of trappers, laden with a year's plews. He had relieved many, through the years, of the burden of trading their furs and getting drunk and catching the clap from one of the red wenches. Morales understood that he would resent having the same thing done to him in the most furious fashion.

Julio turned and whistled shrilly between his fingers. Then he kicked his sorrel into motion and the two horses made their way slowly toward the resting place where Yoder's men had just stopped. The smell of coffee wafted through the air. He and Felipe had used the last of their chickory blend months ago, and he relished the thought of a hot cup before riding on.

As they squatted beside the small fire, tin cups burning their fingers, the liquid scalding their lips, Morales began to pry gently into Yoder's store of information. "Have you met others who go to Rendezvous?" he asked, as if to make conversation.

"Not too many. Most went over the Rockies into the Wasatch and even farther," the big man said. "Did see Prévot and his bunch back in the late fall, though, heading up along the Snake. God knows where they wound up. I tried to spy 'em out, but that damn Prévot is just like a fox.

If he has any notion you're around, you can't fool him or track him."

Julio grunted. He'd had the same problem himself with the canny Frenchman. It was as if he had the second sight—Morales crossed himself without thinking, for he was terrified of anything that smelled like second sight or the evil eye. His early education by the good sisters had gone only so far, giving him fear without its attendant virtues.

"And what of the Bennetts? That man, he have the luck of *el diablo,* I think. Probably he will bring in more plew than all of us together." Morales's tone was bitter.

Yoder spat. "Went west. We didn't see a trace of him this side of the divide. But you're right. Him and that redtail woman and their kid, they're a mean bunch."

Morales almost laughed, for when someone of Yoder's stripe called another mean, it meant they were smarter and tougher than the fur pirate and altogether formidable. He'd learned that already for himself. If Bennett's woman hadn't left him unconscious, he had no doubt that she or her man would have finished him off.

But this year things would change. Morales knew a secret that Cleve Bennett would dislike having betrayed. It was worth a price as well, and if he could not take his vengeance upon the man, the woman, or the child, he would be more shrewd and have his revenge in another and more profitable way.

But Yoder hadn't enough money to become his customer. No, there would be others at the Rendezvous, desperately searching for fresh trapping grounds. Some would have funds, and to one of them he might sell this valuable secret he had learned.

Each year, as the beaver dwindled, there seemed to be more easterners arriving in the mountains, anxious to get into trapping. These days, that was an excellent way to get rid of any money you had to begin with, he thought with amusement.

Morales swallowed the bitter brew, watching the Yoder gang exchanging insults and chews of tobacco. These were men without conscience. Some were also without intelligence, but a man with wit could manage them easily, as he had found with Felipe.

He had thought for years about joining a larger, stronger party, but the idea of subjecting his will to that of some strong leader like Terrebonne had not pleased him. Now, watching Yoder's wide face, in which he could find little sign of intelligence, he wondered if he might work his way into this band, now that it had a new leader.

It should not be difficult to manage Yoder, so subtly that he did not know he was being manipulated. He could guide him, as well as the others, with the same shrewdness he had employed with earlier opponents, who felt themselves to be large frogs in their tiny ponds.

Carville, the second in command, rose and kicked ash over the fire. "Time to git," he said. "The first 'uns to Rendezvous gets the best campsites. And the pick of the gals and the trade goods, too." He snickered, looking aside at Yoder.

Julio rose, too, and turned to help Felipe tighten bits and girths for riding. If he worked his way into this group slowly and cautiously, learning as he went the quirks and foibles of these *perros,* he would soon know if his germinating plan would work.

Few could say that Julio Morales acted without much

forethought. Only that Cheyenne woman who had shamed him before his peers had seen a flaw in his intellect. Never would he make such an error again.

He showed no sign of his thoughts as he fell in behind the huge dun. It was always best to work things out with meticulous care, and it was invariably wise to keep one's own counsel, particularly when dealing with men who would cut your throat without hesitation before or guilt afterward.

Felipe seemed happier now that he had others to talk with as they slouched along the trail. Though it was spring, the wind blew sharply off the heights; occasional light snow sifted down into the forest, laying light burdens on the burgeoning leaves. Even in summer one could run into snow in the mountains, and spring was a fickle season, always.

Yoder led his group along the edges of the slopes, avoiding the higher elevations. He also avoided main trails that might be traveled by any other trappers or Indians heading for the Green and the days of trading. Morales suspected the reason why.

Late one afternoon, as they neared the only trail leading up to the pass, Yoder turned aside into rough country, where he secured his horses and gathered his followers. "A lot of fellows'll be comin' this way soon, goin' to Rendezvous," he said. "Nobody knows we're here. If we kin catch a couple of lone roosters headin' for the henhouse, we'll have even more plews to sell. You with me?"

There was no question of that, of course. Morales smiled, for he had guessed the reason for Yoder's extreme caution as they traveled. Not the most intelligent of men,

Yoder still had a certain crude ability that would serve them all well. If, that is, things went as they planned.

Eventually Morales found himself stationed above the track, behind a clump of boulders whose embedded bases were overgrown with pines and mountain mahogany. Others of the group covered the other bends in the track that climbed to the pass. Among them all, they would be able to finish off anyone planning to take that route to Rendezvous.

Morales understood the art of ambush very well indeed. He and Felipe had taken that option more than once in their time together, but never so obviously and so near to a major gathering of trappers. If this went wrong, and if anyone lived to reach his goal with descriptions of the attackers, the necks of all involved were going to be at risk. He resolved to keep his own face hidden as much as possible, when the time for the ambush arrived.

Yet he was committed. As he listened for the clink of harness metal or the distant snuffle of horses, Julio was tense with anticipation. He liked this; that had been his problem all his life. He was, as his grandfather said when he drove him from the Morales family home in Cuernavaca, a born thief.

That didn't trouble him at all.

When the first rider appeared below, moving around a clump of aspens, Julio twittered like a disturbed bird. Behind and above he heard another call.

He flattened himself behind his boulder, sighting in on the lead rider through a convenient crevice. When the man was well within range, he pulled the trigger.

The roar of the shot echoed up and down the enclosed

track that followed the stream up toward the pass. He peered through the gunsmoke, trying to see if he had hit his target. Close on the heels of that, other shots sounded from above and from the other group. The entire area began to thicken, blue black with smoke of gunpowder.

Hidden by the smoke, Julio slid down the slope beneath his boulders, coming very near to the milling group before anyone saw him. He used his knife to cut the throat of the man he had downed. Around him he heard gasps and grunts and death rattles, and he knew that his companions were also engaged in getting rid of any inconvenient witnesses.

But those they attacked were no greenhorns, it was clear, for three of them had put their horses together in a fast-moving wedge, forcing a way through the struggling men on the trail. Julio saw this happen through a gap in the smoke, caused by the fitful breeze.

He moved around the milling men, hoping to intercept the escapees before they knew he was there. Behind him he heard a deep groan. It sounded like Yoder, he thought as he slipped downward to land in a clump of serviceberry.

The riders were now farther down the track, heading toward the flat country . . . too far for him to catch. He comforted himself with the thought that all the confusion would have prevented anyone from seeing the attackers closely enough to identify individuals.

He turned and climbed back toward the fight, but by the time he reached the scene of the ambush, all was quiet. Four strangers lay sprawled in the dust, their blood steaming in the cold mountain air.

Off to one side three of Yoder's men crouched about a recumbent shape, huge and ungainly. Yoder, for certain.

Julio went to kneel beside the big man. "You are hurt, *sí*?" he asked.

The pale eyes opened, but Yoder's stare did not see him. "Shit!" the fur pirate gasped. Then his head lolled sideways and blood drooled from the corner of his mouth.

Julio Cardenas Morales arranged his face in a suitable expression of sorrow. *"Es muerto."* He sighed, crossing himself. "We must bury him, I think. And those others. No one must know that there has been trouble here. Those who escape have seen nothing of us, and we must know nothing of them, *es verdad*?"

Carville, who seemed too stunned to think, rose to his feet. Julio thought he seemed relieved to find someone doing the thinking, with Yoder dead.

"Yeah. I'll git some of the boys right on it. What about the horses, though? Everybody knows everybody else's horses, seems as if." It was somewhat surprising that he had thought of that problem.

Julio thought for a long moment. That was true. If they came to Rendezvous leading horses laden with plews, and if anyone there recognized those horses as belonging to the dead men, whoever they might be, things could become most uncomfortable.

"Load ours heavily. Loose the others and drive them far away. There is no time to dig the grave large enough for so many horses. Put our friend Ben on top of the others in the hole. To honor him, *sí*?"

To his relief, no one questioned his orders. Felipe, glad to be one of a group again, worked alongside the others as they dug a deep grave far back on the side of the mountain where a rocky ledge had caught centuries of soil washing down the slopes. When the corpses had been interred, after being well and thoroughly robbed in the process, the group turned to Julio for further orders.

He smiled. "We have lost a good friend in Ben Yoder," he said. Carville nodded. "But if you like, I, who am known for wit and shrewdness in trade and . . . other things . . . will lead you. We will go to Rendezvous with all these plew and we will return rich men. You agree?"

Their murmur of agreement filled his heart with wicked glee. This was the beginning that he had planned, come to pass without any effort on his part. The future had begun to look bright, and he intended for it to become even brighter.

chapter

—3—

The site of Rendezvous was already beginning to fill up when Second Son followed the last packhorse down into the confusion at the bottom of the steep trail. Cleve, riding ahead with Joe Ferris, was already whooping greetings to old acquaintances, his voice lost in the bedlam below. She could see a number of people she knew amid the dust and the smoke of the many fires.

The sprawl of tipis in the bottom of the valley held, Second Son noted, the camp of Sun Turns Red, his painted symbol glowing crimson in the sunlight. Even as she turned her gaze toward the trading sheds, she recognized Ed Fellmore and Lee Pulliam. She looked about for Tom Carson, who had been the third party in the men's earlier trapping venture, but nowhere could she see him.

Billy-Wolf, just behind her on Blaze, moved up beside her as the path widened. He, too, recognized old acquaintances. "Can I go up there with Papa?" he asked in his quiet little voice. "I would like to speak with Mr. Fellmore and Mr. Pulliam."

She nodded and smiled. He and his father always enjoyed this annual get-together of trappers and traders to the fullest. Second Son, on the other hand, was inevitably under considerable strain, trying to keep a low profile.

She had learned the hard way that these men felt threatened by a woman as strong and dangerous as they themselves were. She wanted no killing, if it could be avoided, particularly since she had a son to protect. Her encounter with Morales had left her with a bitterness in her heart that had never quite eased.

As the boy rode ahead to join his father, she chivied the packhorses uphill to a likely campsite, well above the stink and smoke of the main camp and not too far from the place where a spring bubbled out of solid rock. She tethered the animals while she unloaded their bales of plews.

She and Cleve had learned that a loaded packhorse was far too easy to drive or lead away; if the thief was caught, he always showed a broken rope and claimed he found the beast wandering, and nobody could prove him a liar. For that reason, she always unloaded their animals at once, so nothing of the kind could happen.

Once she had the bales stacked and roped together to a tree, she began raising the tipi. Before she was well begun,

Cleve joined her, and together they put up their shelter and found stones for their fire pit. This was such familiar work that they didn't speak as they put up the shelter, but once the fire was going well, its bed of coals growing nicely, Cleve produced a fresh haunch of venison.

Second Son stared at it. They had not hunted for a hand of days, traveling on their dried stocks of food.

Cleve chuckled. "Old Emile sent it to you as a gift. He and his boys just pulled in, loaded with meat. Hell, they have more deer and elk than beaver, seems like. We'll have to eat most of it, though. Billy-Wolf and Ferris will probably be over there half the night and they'll come back stuffed to their limits."

With the trained ear of a longtime spouse, Second Son heard the undercurrent of wistfulness in her man's voice. "You go, too, if you wish. I will roast the meat, and we will have it already cooked for several days to come. Then I will arrange things in the tipi so that when you return all will be ready for sleep."

His pale eyes brightened. He reached out and pulled her into a bear hug. "You are a dandy, Second Son. You know that?"

She smiled. "I know that you think that, which is all I need to understand. Now go and talk with your old friends. I shall finish setting up camp and then I may rest for a time."

She did not add that she might also find a spot from which she could check out the entire Rendezvous area. If any of her old foes were attending this year, she wanted to know where they camped and what they were doing. She had learned the hard way to take such steps in order to avoid them.

Accidental meetings when they were among other trappers were unavoidable, but with other people about it was easy to sidestep trouble. She did not intend for any other sort to arise.

Cleve moved down the slope toward the trading huts, leaving her to consider this year's harvest of furs. No, it was not a bountiful one. They were going to have to return to their early trapping ground, that hidden valley high in the Absarokas, with its almost impossible approach. Otherwise she could see that their trapping days were about to end.

She secured the bales, knowing that it would be tomorrow before Cleve would begin taking them down and start his serious bartering. He had a reputation for producing top-grade furs, and after so many years there were traders who saved the best of their goods to show him.

He, in turn, had become a sharp bargainer. In addition, he always held back a solid sum in gold that no Rendezvous foolishness ever succeeded in getting out of his hands. The extra gold was stored in a cave both of them knew, concealed beneath the winter bed of a particularly large grizzly.

She finished her work. Then she streaked her face with a pattern of dirt, wrapped herself in a dark deerhide robe, and covered her glossy hair with an old hat, a turkey feather drooping from its band.

She looked, she knew, like one of the Indian hangers-on who haunted the Rendezvous, cadging whiskey and running errands for the trappers. In such a guise, she could go where she liked without being noticed, which was exactly what she intended.

As she moved along the slope other trappers were setting up camp, cursing and laughing and already, some of them well on their way to drunkenness. The traders always had some liquor for early arrivals, and she understood why. A drunken trapper was far easier to swindle than a sober one. She was thankful that Cleve had learned early that he could not drink very much without becoming terribly sick.

A burly fellow stumbled across her path. She stepped aside, belched loudly, and asked him for whiskey. That sent him away promptly, for nobody liked the sort of Indian she was pretending to be. They did not understand, as she did, that some of those seemingly incapacitated warriors were alert, intent upon learning for their people exactly what the white men planned.

Second Son chuckled softly as she went on her way. A drunken Indian, she well knew, was seldom as intoxicated as he seemed. His ears were honed to sharpness, and he usually understood much more English than he admitted. That was one advantage of having adversaries who were, many of them, convinced that red-skinned people were children.

She had realized, during the years of her association with Cleve's people, that they did not understand the sharp, practical wisdom of the different tribes with whom they dealt. The old chiefs, sitting about the fires in their tipis with white trappers, did more than smoke the pipe and talk of trivialities with their pale-eyed associates. Those leaders were skilled at judging men of all kinds, even white ones. They understood more about those who came from the east than any white man, even Cleve, would believe.

She had seen the Blackfoot and the Dakotah, the Kiowa

and the Absaroka and the Pawnee send such scouts into gatherings like this. Most of her own Cheyenne people still stood proudly aloof from Rendezvous, but she reported all she learned to her brother Singing Wolf of the Burning Heart Cheyenne, when she had the opportunity. He conveyed important things to the other bands, when he saw the need.

She was no spy, and yet she was Cheyenne. There was a sad feeling inside her that one day there would be need for her people to understand and to think ahead of these uncontrolled and numerous white men.

Ahead, a new group of trappers was making their way into the camp. A familiar turn of the head, as the one in front spoke to the man behind him, brought Second Son up short. She melted into a pine thicket, from which she stared at the oncoming riders. The leader was Julio Morales, without any doubt.

Now what was that one doing with such a large band? She noted Felipe, his old companion, well back among the other twice-double-handful of riders. Then she began recognizing others: Carville, who was second in command to Ben Yoder. LeBoeuf, Dennis, Thatcher, Patrick . . . she drew a sharp breath.

Most of those riding behind Morales were longtime members of Jules Terrebonne's gang of fur thieves. Yoder had succeeded to the leadership after Terrebonne's disappearance, but there was no sign of him among these newcomers.

So how had Morales become a leader, as he obviously seemed, of this bunch of villains?

She and Cleve were the only ones who knew that they had killed Terrebonne, themselves, years ago when Billy-

Wolf was born. No one else understood what had become of him, and it was agreed that even their son would never know.

It was impossible to guess what men of that stripe might do in retaliation, even though there was little loyalty among them. Cleve and Second Son kept their secret and never mentioned it, even between themselves.

Interesting that Morales had joined that group, in particular. But she had others to locate, and as she went about doing that she thought hard about her discovery.

Others would, of course, notice very quickly that the leadership of this gang had changed. What troubled her was an intuition that it meant even more problems for the already troubled trappers in the Rockies. Add Morales's unmistakable intelligence to the strength and ruthlessness of that group, and you had the makings of hard times for everyone.

But she set that thought aside at last, having spotted those she intended to avoid. Tonight, when Cleve at last came to the tipi, she would talk with him about this new development.

Though he had prevented her killing Morales, that had been to avoid being forbidden to come to Rendezvous in the future. She knew that her husband would kill the Mexican himself, if there was ever fresh cause and an opportunity.

She started back up the slope, walking with careful steps, like one who distrusted his liquor-fuddled reflexes. Under the brim of the wide hat, her eyes noted everything that moved among the trees. Never again would she be surprised by drunken men intent upon mischief.

A shape, with leaf shade dappled across her leather

dress, appeared off to her right, and Second Son watched unobtrusively as she passed. Otter Woman, the oldest wife of Sun Turns Red, was gathering herbs before the men from the camps trampled them. Other women, young and middle-aged, were also gleaning what could be found on the slopes above the river.

They did not look up as this "man" passed, and Second Son sighed. What would it have been like to be a woman, busy from dawn to night with providing food, shelter, healing, clothing for a family? She would never know, for to her own people she was a man, as surely as the aspect she now presented.

To the Burning Hearts, Cleve was her wife, captured fairly in battle. A chuckle rose again into her throat as she turned her steps toward her own tipi.

To her surprise, the fire had been replenished and Joe Ferris sat beside it, turning the venison haunch on its thong as it hung from the tripod over the coals. Fragrant drips of juice spattered into the blaze, and Second Son felt suddenly hungry.

Smiling, she stepped into camp. Ferris looked up, alarmed, his hand on his flintlock, until she removed her hat and let her dark braid fall down to her shoulders.

"I can't never get used to you, gal. You can do anything I can—'cept maybe one—just about as good as anybody I ever see. You can look as much like one of them drunk old Injuns as they do theirselves. What you been doin' in that getup?"

She laid aside the blanket and the hat, wiped her face with some of the water from her ever-present pot, and sat cross-legged across the fire from him. "I must see who is here," she told him. "I will not make trouble if it can be helped. So I find their camps, those who have tried to best me, and I do not pass near them."

He laughed delightedly. "That's the way it is with the good ones. I've seed fellers so tough that nobody can whip 'em, any way, anyhow, but mostly they don't go out pickin' fights. They sidestep trouble, not haulin' it up to their camp. You're just the same, Second Son."

She felt that he had paid her a compliment. Smiling, she rose to cut a slab of meat from the haunch and offered it to him on one of her improvised wood-split platters. Then, sitting on her heels, she ate with him as the night sounds of Rendezvous began rising from below.

There was a drum throbbing in the Pawnee camp at the edge of the valley, and someone was chanting. From time to time a girl shrieked or a man shouted obscenities. But in general the sound was that of talk, deep man-voices catching up on a year of work and danger.

Second Son would gladly have sent their plews by someone else and avoided this meeting, for she knew it held dangers for her that her husband would never understand. Yet it seemed that white men must get together and brag and curse and get their fill of talk and whiskey at least once a year.

For her part, she could live contentedly with only her own family, without even her clan and tribe. She had wondered for a long time about that difference, and she had decided that it had less to do with red men and white than with men and women and their very different needs.

Ferris belched and sighed. "Good old Emile. Him and me talked for a good long while this evenin'. Caught up on a lot of things. And that meat is plumb welcome. Tomorrow I'll go out and get us a couple of woodchucks or a deer, if they've not all been scared over the mountains by this noise. But now I'll turn in, Second Son. Bet them boys of yours don't come for a while yet!" He yawned and went into the tipi, where she heard the rustle of his bedroll.

Of all the white men she had known, there were a few—less than a handful, actually—who had been her true friends. Holy William, who had died the night her son was born, had been the first, and she still remembered his strange, mad sweetness with wonder.

Joe Ferris was her staunch ally, even though in general he did not like or trust women. Emile Prévot, whom she had never known well, made it plain that this wife of his friend was also a friend, who could turn to him if there was need. Paul Levreaux, even less well known to her, was still to be trusted, in a pinch.

Not many, she thought, for the number of white-eyes she had met in her years of coming to Rendezvous. Her enemies, on the other hand, were many. Most were not openly against her, but she could see in the slant-eyed looks they gave her that many of these men felt threatened because of her mere existence.

It could not be remedied. She moved the haunch, now done, into the higher branches of a nearby pine and secured it above the reach of any adventuresome bear. Then she, too, went into the tipi and rolled herself in her fur blanket.

Cleve and Billy-Wolf would come when they came. She would sleep now.

chapter

—4—

Malachi Walters was a small, slight man who looked to be no match for those who hired him as a guide or, these past two years, chose to trap alongside him. He found it good policy to be soft-spoken, but it amused him to know that he could beat the socks off just about any mountain man who decided to bully him. More than one had tried, back a long time ago when he was a greenhorn, and not one of them ever tried it again. His thin frame held a wiry strength that fooled even the best of them.

For two years he had been associated with Ben Beeville,

who had, two years ago, led a group of trappers up the Snake. Something else, Walters felt certain, had been involved in that expedition, but between poor trapping and raids by Blackfoot Indians, it had not been a season to remember with any pleasure or profit.

Though he had not trapped these mountains in the early days, as many here had done, he had talked with enough of the old-timers to get an idea of the way things used to be. He knew that the Rockies, by and large, were trapped out. His group was coming to Rendezvous with twenty-three packs of plews, and that was ridiculous for the time and manpower expended in getting them.

He came down from the north, Beeville's long train of packhorses and men strung out behind him, and as he rode he thought hard about the future. Most of the men he knew took each day at a time, never thinking ahead. But Walters knew that if the fur trade was to survive, someone must find new trapping territory. That might just work in with whatever secret mission Beeville was engaged in, too.

Walters did not intend to remain a trapper, of course. He had spent a large part of his life as a scout, explorer, and guide, and that life appealed to him. He had traveled through new territory before this, and he had an idea he'd like to sit in the warm sun old Jed Smith had described as shining always on the California country. There were many ways for a smart man to make a living, and, as usual, he was hankering after something new and different.

So when that line of men and horses pulled into Rendezvous, he left Freeman Douglas, Beeville's second in command, and the others to make arrangements and went to look up Emile Prévot. The Frenchman always beat him to the gathering, and he knew nobody more qualified to help him find for Beeville the necessary men to go on a long journey. It was time to map a way to the coastal mountains and the Pacific Ocean, by way of an easier trail than any now known.

He found Prévot easily. His string of French curses rose on the air like smoke, and interested men were homing in on the center of the dispute.

"You tell me I bring the poor plew? *Vous êtes fou!* I tell you that you bring the poor trade good, *espèce de cochon!* These whiskey, it is water." He spat a long stream into the small fire beside the trader's shanty. As if to prove his point, there was more steam than flame where the stuff hit the hot coals.

"These knife, it is like the tin, not the good steel. You trade for my plew? You will do better than this, *mon ami*, or I go elsewhere!"

Walters grinned. This was an annual ritual, much appreciated by everyone. When all possible insults had been traded, Cash Younger would offer a more reasonable deal, and the Frenchman, after much complaint, would accept it. But the entertainment provided by their different trading styles was fun for all. Sometimes it ended in a free-for-all, which was even more enjoyable.

Walters leaned against a tree, waiting for the trade to be made, but he kept an eye on all who passed. There was Ben Yoder's lieutenant, Carville, with his henchmen. It was a mystery what had happened to their old boss, Jules Terrebonne, but Malachi doubted that anyone would ever solve it. He suspected that Yoder himself might have had a hand in Terrebonne's disappearance. Not that anyone cared—if anyone deserved being bushwhacked, it was the French fur pirate.

That Mexican Morales seemed to be part of the bunch this year. That was interesting, and Walters filed it away as something that might be important, down the line.

Beyond them he looked over to the farther slope of a deep ravine. There he caught the glint of yellow hair beneath the edge of a fur hat. Only one man had hair that color, and he straightened and yelled, "Cleve!" so loudly that even the bickering traders forgot their argument.

The tall fellow turned and smiled once he saw who had called. They headed for a point at the top of the ravine and perched together on a stump, ready to renew a friendship that had begun by chance when Walters stumbled into the Bennett trapping camp back in his wandering days.

"You look prime," Malachi said to the younger man. "We did pretty good, but not like the old-timers tell me it used to be."

"It's gone soft all over the map," Cleve replied. "Time we found some new country, or else Second Son and I may go back to her folks out in the Plains."

Walters shook his head. "You don't want to, boy. Things is going to hot up now that so many of our kind are comin' west. Stands to reason the Indians are going to object to having their land took and their game goin' into the bellies of white men's children. I can see a time when it won't be safe to be in even a Cheyenne village. Even though your in-laws avoid trouble with our kind, there's many that will kill any Indian he sees, just because they're redskins."

Regretfully Cleve nodded.

"White men can't understand anybody who won't let 'em take what they want," Malachi went on. "You know as well as I do that it makes them tarnally mad when they don't get their way without a fight."

Cleve's eyes looked bleak. "Already there's been friction. My brother-in-law says a bunch of easterners had trouble with some Pawnee last summer, upriver from the Burning Hearts. They came roaring down on his village, looking for blood, and it was only because the hunters hadn't gone far and heard the yells and the shots that they got there in time to save our people from being massacred. That's not going to make things safe and peaceful, if it keeps on."

Bennett's face became even grimmer. "If they get the Cheyenne set against 'em, our kind's going to wish it had never happened. They think they've got trouble with the other tribes? They don't know *anybody* as tough as the Cheyenne."

He shook his head, his yellow hair flopping against his ears. "I can see blood on the land, before it's all over. I just hope . . . I just hope my son won't be the one to suffer because of all this."

Malachi felt a bit uncomfortable at mentioning the expedition that he and Beeville were putting together, but Cleve and his wife would be great additions to his number, if they would come. Their son was a bit young for such a trip, but surely he'd be safe with his uncle, for it was early yet and plans still had to be made.

"I've got a deal I'm helping Beeville organize," he said. "You might be interested, being as trapping has got so slack. We intend to map a new route to California, going north of the Great Salt Lake. Ought to be a lot safer and easier than Jed Smith's desert trail. You and your woman'd be mighty welcome. We're goin' to need people that know how to travel light and hang tough."

Cleve looked at him closely, and Walters could see him considering the proposal. Then he shook his head, a bit sadly. "No, I guess not. We've got a secret trapping ground we've kept for just such a time. We want to go back there this winter."

He paused for a long moment. Then he said, his tone wistful, "But it sounds like fun, anyway. I may just use your new map one of these days, if you get through and come back to share it around."

Walters sighed. But he knew that many others had no such reserve against hard times and there would be no trouble in getting some thirty or forty men to travel to California. It was plain that this Rendezvous was seeing poor hauls for just about everyone there.

He sighed heavily. "Looks as if things just keep changing, whether you want 'em to or not."

Cleve leaned back against a nearby pine and guffawed. "You know you like changes better than most, Malachi," he said, wiping his eyes on his sleeve. "How many places have you been to and seen and done, just because you can't stand to keep still in one spot, doing the same thing, day after day?"

Walters grinned reluctantly. He might fool some of these fellows who spent their winters in the mountains talking to bears, but Cleve Bennett was a smart man. It had taken a while for him to understand just how smart. But once he got to know the Bennetts, Walters had realized that this one had more book learning than a lot of teachers back home. That, added to his quick wits, made him formidable.

Besides that, he had a wife who could make anybody stand up and take notice, even if the Cheyenne thought she was a man, which she definitely wasn't. He'd listened to other trappers, and those who hated her the most were the ones who unwittingly said the most in her favor.

She bowed her neck to no one. She was faithful to her husband. She could lick anyone, anytime, when it was a fair fight, though she was under middle height and lacked reach. Still, she was smart enough to work around her limitations and to use the size and strength of her opponents against them.

"I sure would like to see you and your wife come with me," he said. "But I can see that you have your own business to tend to." He glanced downhill at the trading shed. The two who had been dickering had settled up and Prévot was moving along the trail toward another knot of trappers.

"I'd better go talk to Emile. He'll know who's ripe to change their scenery and find new ground. You be keerful, you hear?" He felt Cleve's gaze on his back as he descended to intercept the Frenchman on the path.

Prévot greeted him with a bear hug that threatened to crack his ribs. "You have return with the great haul, *n'est-ce pas*?" the Frenchman asked, but his tone said that he knew better. He set the smaller man on his feet again and waited, arms akimbo, for his reply.

Walters chuckled. "You know better than that, Emile. Nobody here got more than a skimpy little batch this time around. Except for them." He gestured toward the loose cluster of men who had come in with Carville and the Mexican Morales.

"They seem to have lucked into somethin' special, don't

you think?" His tone was quizzical, but he left an edge of suspicion in it.

Prévot shook his grizzled head, making the tail that had been left on his wolverine cap swing wildly. "Those men, they are the thief and murderer, we all know too well. What happen to Ben Yoder they do not say plain, but I know them. I have know them for many year, and I smell"—he tapped his gnarled nose—"something that is rotten."

He looked thoughtful. "My own thought is that they attack someone who now lies in the mountains staring at the vulture, eh? And the fur that man trap come on to Rendezvous without him."

"They've got packs of plews up to here," Walters said. "I saw them unloadin' down there. It took more than one trapper to catch that many, if I'm a judge. Who ain't come in yet?"

A furrow appeared between the Frenchman's brows. "Bridwell, he have not come. Snakewhip MacNew I have not see. That new one from *Angleterre*—what is the name? Constable. No, I have not see him, too. But we are early, *n'est-ce pas*?"

Malachi shook his head doubtfully. "Good men get here early, I been told. Bridwell and MacNew are good men. What you suppose made 'em late?"

But that was speculation, and he shrugged away the problem and drew Prévot aside. "You camped yet?" he asked. "I've got something on that you may be interested in. And I'm goin' to need men. Quite a few really good ones, in fact."

As he talked he saw the Frenchman's deep-sunk eyes

brighten. Prévot nodded frequently, adding comments along the way.

When Malachi was done, Emile gave a great *whoosh* of a sigh. "You and Beeville have the good notion, I think. There mus' be fresh mountain, many valley, fine trap and hunt, there to the west.

"Why Smith, he tell me that he have make that journey, more than once, though it was terrible and dry and he lose much horse along the way and many men. That first route he would not recommend to his enemy, he say, much less a friend. But what he find there promise much, if a better route can be map, I think."

As it was Smith's letter to William Clark that had interested Beeville in locating a new route west to the ocean, Walters nodded. "You're right as rain," he said. "Now help me find some men who'll want to help us do just that."

Prévot stared off across the valley below his camp. "There will be many, I think," he said. "And I will help with that, *oui*? Indeed, I would like to go with you, as well. The trap, it is too hard now, and I grow *fatigué*. Me, I get too old for a journey like that."

His smile was bright as a new penny, and Walters knew that he had gained a valuable ally, if not a companion on his expedition.

chapter
—5—

The babble of talk, the smell of liquor and men and horses, the excitement of Rendezvous always stimulated Cleve. He didn't drink more than a friendly gulp or two, and his wife would not put up with his visiting the women in the tipis in the valley, but that really didn't count. It was the company of other white men that he craved.

Many were incoherent with drink, of course, and those he ignored. But the few he really liked and respected, Prévot and Walters, Bridwell and Constable and their ilk, were a different story. With them he would sit for hours around the fire, exchanging news and tall tales and bullshit. There was nothing better, for this short time in the year, than reacquainting himself with the interests of his own kind.

Now he sat on a chunk of firewood beside Emile's campfire, wondering idly why Bridwell and Constable were so late in getting to Rendezvous. Billy-Wolf, always ready to sit in, silent and bright-eyed, on the talk of his elders, leaned against his shoulder.

Even the boy, Cleve realized, understood the tenor of the quiet talk around the circle of men. Things were not good. Beaver young and old had been taken in the past decade, and now many dams lay broken, without any beaver to repair them.

Too many lodges stood empty in drying ponds incapable of protecting them. Even where there were colonies left, they were small, the animals hardly worth setting traps for.

"Give ten year," Prévot was saying, "and the beaver, he is gone. No fur trade, except for the occasional lynx or fox or such. It is time, *mes amis,* that we look to other work. Or"—he glanced about the circle quickly—"other place, eh?"

Cleve didn't allow himself to smile, but he knew that Walters had approached the Frenchman to help him fill the roster of men for his California expedition. If he and Second Son had not so carefully preserved that hidden pair of valleys in the Absarokas for just such a time of need, he would have been interested in this project himself.

They visited their secret spot almost every summer, to make sure that no one had yet discovered that it was possible to get men and horses down the seemingly impossible cliffs. Yet they had not trapped there since Billy-Wolf was a toddler. Thought for the future was something that too few of his fellows here at Rendezvous seemed to understand, but it would stand his family in good stead this coming winter.

He was half dozing as Emile explained the trip to California to the interested group at his fire. "You have hear, most of you, what Smith he have say about that country. Sun and wine and sleepy mission, *oui*? Young Spanish women of great beauty, as well. Only the coast seem to be recognize by the Spaniard as valuable. The mountain, except for the occasional redskin, lie untrap, unhunt, waiting for our hand."

Eyes brightened and several of the loungers sat up straighter. "And Beeville is goin' to run this outfit? I hear he's got some kind of gov'ment job, along with his reg'lar trappin'," said Mud Kinney. "I run into one of the Brits from Fort Vancouver, back a ways last year, and he was all upset about what he called American spies comin' into their territory."

"Perhaps," said Prévot. "But this time he go to the west, not the north. The Spanish, they are not so demanding. They allow Smith an' his men to remain without the official permit, until they rest and replace the horse.

"Smith, he promise to return as he have come, but that route, he claim, is ver' bad, so he come back another way. The official on the coast, they do not even send the scout to make certain he keep his word."

Cleve grinned then. He'd talked to Smith himself a while back. What Prévot said was quite true, and it showed how wide open the country was, if people decided to cross the distances to claim it. California was a long way from Spain. Hell, it was a long way from Mexico City, too, and officials who might make trouble.

It did sound tempting. He'd been trapping since he was twenty, and the thought of going away from the familiar ranges along the Rockies, crossing new country, seeing new people was very attractive.

But there was Billy-Wolf. It was too hard a trip for a boy.

The others were talking quietly, considering this venture, when there came three shots from the hill leading down to the trading sheds. Dogs began barking in the Indian camps below, and Cleve heard shouts and loud voices approaching. He rose quickly and turned, followed by everyone there, toward the spot from which the noise came.

Billy-Wolf was at his heels, and it occurred to him that this might not be a safe place for his son. "You go to Second Son," he said. "Tell her to keep watch—something is happening down there."

Without a protest, though Cleve knew the boy was longing to see what was going on, his son turned up the path leading to their own camp. Joe Ferris would be there, and with the old man on guard with Second Son, nobody was going to get to the boy.

Cleve rushed down the path, scanning the forested slopes around him, watching those who were also moving toward the sheds. When he came nearer, he recognized a voice. Jim Bridwell! By God, that was his old crony from the Ashworth trapping days, come at last.

Emile pushed up beside him. "It is Bridwell, eh? Now I wonder why he shoot, why he yell? That man, he is always quiet, always control. But we see in a moment, *oui*?"

When they pushed into the crowd around the trading sheds, Cleve saw that three men, still mounted, were in the center of the confusion. Bridwell, of course. Even in the fire-reddened dimness, there was no mistaking that long-boned frame. Who else? Constable? Yes. And a third, slumping forward on his mount's neck as if wounded.

"Here, let me through," he said. Something in his tone made the excited trappers make way for him, and soon he found himself beside the horses. The dark hat had flopped over the face of the wounded man, but when he raised his head to see who was lifting him from the saddle, Cleve saw his face.

"Paul!" he exclaimed. "Paul Levreaux! What happened to you boys, anyway?"

With a grunt of pain, the Frenchman slid into Cleve's grasp, and the big trapper half lifted him over to a log bench against the shed wall. Blood streaked the leather shirt, the fringed leggings, and the long-boned hands of his old friend.

"I am shoot, *mon ami.* Bushwhackers, up on the South Pass. We join together to make the trip to Rendezvous, but now most of those we travel with lie dead, I think. Only we three escape." He stifled a groan as Cleve sliced through the tough hide of his shirt to reveal a puckered wound, now clotted but draining pus.

Cash Younger came up beside the two and stared down at Levreaux. "Bridwell tells me you fellows met some fur thieves up a ways. See anybody you recognized?" The man's voice was tight, his fury controlled but obvious.

Cleve understood why. If such things happened too often, it might well destroy the Rendezvous as an institution. Those who made small fortunes every summer bringing trade goods from the east would find themselves driven to another trade, safer, perhaps, but far less profitable.

Levreaux shook his head, making the hat flap. "We go along the trail, everything quiet and peaceful. We watch close, but suddenly the shot come, many together, and most of our band lie dead or struggle on the groun'.

"Our frien' Jim Bridwell, he call together those of us still mount, and we make the run for it, all together. The horse, she push aside the man who try to stop us, an' we shoot at others. But the smoke, she was so thick we cannot see to aim."

"You lose many plews?" Younger asked, his tone somewhat odd.

"Fifty pack we lose, among us. That is the work for ten men for the winter. Not a good harvest, no."

Cleve felt a jolt of anger. "That bunch that used to be Terrebonne's—they came in with a big batch of bales. Too many for the size of their band these days. Ben Yoder wasn't with 'em, either. I wonder—"

"But we can't prove a thing," Younger said. "Their horses are really theirs. We sort of looked over the string once they were unloaded, and not a one didn't belong to the Yoder band. A plew is a plew, and nobody has found a way yet to tell one from another." He sounded suspicious and disgusted, both at once.

There was a whisper of air, and Cleve looked up to see his wife. Second Son bent over the wounded man. "You would like to take him to our tipi?" she asked. "I am no real healer, but I understand wounds. And Ferris is very good, too. We can help Paul better than these drunken men."

At Cleve's nod, she and Younger eased their hands beneath the feverish body of the Frenchman. Emile, stepping out of the crowd, also helped as they moved carefully along the trail, up the slope to their camp.

"I do not like these thing," Prévot muttered into Cleve's ear. "I think it is more than time to go away from these mountain to a new place."

As Cleve waited outside his lodge for Second Son and Ferris to do their work, he thought of what Prévot had said. More and more he was feeling in his gut that his time in the mountains was ending. Yet he wanted as badly as his wife did to return to that deep, dim-lit valley, hidden by overhanging spruces and firs and mountain mahogany that concealed the terrible drop down its stony sides.

Without Second Son's remembrance of being shown that secret place by her brother when she was a very young warrior, he would never have dreamed it was there. Singing Wolf had told his young warrior-sister to recall it in time of danger, and it had saved them and their unborn son from the warriors who hunted them.

He sighed, and Emile Prévot, smoking his pipe on the other side of the fire, grunted. "This is not the good time, eh, Cleve? I feel a strangeness in the bone. The *pressentiment*—what you call the hunch—it tell me that things have change too much.

"The time for us here is pass, *mon ami,* and it will not return. I myself will not go with M'sieur Beeville an' his group, for I am no longer the *jeune homme* I was. But I will go someplace new, fresh. Perhaps the Canada. I think perhaps my old frien' Paul would go west, if he had not been hurt."

Joe Ferris stooped through the door hole of the tipi and

stood before the fire, stretching. As Cleve looked up at him he nodded reassuringly. "He's goin' to make it. Just went through the muscle of his upper arm. Missed the artery.

"Too tough, these Frenchies, to kill with one bullet, ain't they, Emile? How many chunks of lead have been took out of your hide over the years?"

Prévot laughed. Billy-Wolf, who had been dozing, his head in the man's lap, was suddenly alert. "You've been shot, Mr. Prévot? Really?"

"About twenty time is all. Never in the stomach, *mon petit.* Shoot one of my kin' in the head, it give the small headache. In the foot, we limp for a bit. But shoot in the stomach so we cannot eat and we die at once. Or . . . elsewhere . . . so we cannot appreciate the beautiful woman. Then we die, too."

Relieved, Cleve chuckled, knowing that there was more truth than fantasy in the Frenchman's words. Before he could speak, Second Son came out of the tipi, her face sweaty, her hands full of bloody moss, which was her usual packing for stopping bleeding wounds.

"It did not do him terrible damage," she said, putting the damp mess on the fire and watching the resulting sputter and steam. "His arm will be well in time, I think.

"Watch him well," she said to Prévot. "Do not let him do much for some days. And make him drink—not the liquor but water. I have noticed that when warriors lose much blood, they need much liquid to replace it."

It made sense. Prévot went into the tipi, spoke softly with his old friend, and came out ready to take Levreaux down to the big camp that the old companions usually shared. As he trudged solidly down the slope, with Paul clinging to him and doing his best to walk firmly, Cleve felt a surge of affection.

They might be rough, cruel when necessary, but those two Frenchmen were as good friends as he would ever know. Too bad he and they couldn't go west . . . but he pushed away the thought. There would be time later to explore that endless country toward the sunset.

chapter
6

Lawrence Biddle was disgusted. He'd come west from New Hampshire with visions of using his inheritance from his father to make a fortune in furs. To his dismay, he found that other entrepreneurs had been there before him, and all his Yankee trading skills were useless. The cream of this business had already been skimmed.

He'd bought traps and supplies and gone off into the wilderness to try his own hand at catching beaver, but he found only territory that had been trapped out. His take, representing a year's work, was pitiful, and he knew that it would hardly pay for supplies to tide him over for another winter.

If he hadn't quarreled so terribly with his brother over dividing the estate, he might have decided to go home again. He'd make more clerking in the store his grandfather had established than at trapping, it was becoming clear.

His inherited cash, stashed around his belly in a money belt, was not something he intended to dig into for supplies. He'd change directions before he would spend his hard-won heritage on this fool's game. Only if he could find a new territory, as yet untapped by beaver hunters, did he stand a chance of succeeding.

Biddle was as hardheaded as any Yankee ever born. To admit he had made a mistake was unthinkable; he was doing his best to locate fresh streams with relatively fresh sources of plews. To that end he had questioned everyone he could buttonhole at the Rendezvous, asking not-too-subtle questions about the luck of other individuals and groups. It seemed that everyone there had been around for years and knew everyone else well.

When he sidled into a group of drinking, cursing, back-slapping men, they seemed to avoid him, as if he were an intruder. He'd tried talking with Indians as well, but he hadn't learned to understand their pidgin English. They, if anyone, could have told him what he wanted to know, but he often thought that even the savages were laughing at him.

He traded in his pitiful haul for as much as he could squeeze out of Cash Younger, which was more than Younger liked but less than Biddle wanted. He managed to wangle a jug out of the trader, too, and that he took over into the shelter of a spinney of alder and sat down to drink himself blind.

He was about half-seas-over when someone sat beside him and leaned against the alder stump he was using as a backrest. "You did not do well, my friend," said a pleasant voice with a Mexican accent. "Too many have the same situation this season, I think."

"Dammit, I heard that a man could make fortunes out here. But that time must be past. I couldn't find a damn beaver stream with enough animals to make trapping worthwhile," he said, proud that he was able to speak clearly, even with so much whiskey inside him.

"There are still the streams that have not been trapped," said that insinuating voice. "I know of a valley, not too far, that is so steep, so hidden, so hard to find that no one except its discoverer has gone there."

"Why ain't you trapped it yourself?" Biddle snapped. "I can't figure there being anything left that hasn't been swarmed over by these unwashed bastards." He realized that his voice was getting loud, and he tried to get himself in hand.

"Oh, there is," said the Mexican. "I have followed the gringo and his *puta* when they go to check on their secret place. If I had not followed, I would never have find it, it is true. Once they have gone away, I go down into the valley, at much peril of my life, believe me, and there I find a stream, many lodges, many beaver."

"Then you're a fool if you didn't haul in your traps and skim off the cream," Biddle muttered.

"I have grown weary of trapping. By nature, I am a lazy man, and the trapping, it is the great labor. It is time I go back to Cuernavaca and live like the civilize person again.

So I will sell to you the secret I hold. If, that is, you wish to come to the next Rendezvous loaded with the rich plew, while the rest of these *perros* bring the light pack and the long face." The dark eyes were bright, and the man spoke well.

Biddle laughed, choked, and sputtered. When he had his breath again, he said, "You are trying to cheat a New Hampshire man. We don't buy a thing without seeing, smelling, and biting it to make sure it's real and solid. If you've got such a place, you show it to me. Then I'll pay you, if I think it's worth what you ask." He squinted at the oval face, which seemed a bit blurred.

"I am ask five hundred Yankee dollar for this secret. A small price, for there is trap for many winter in this place. One man, he will work for a long while before it is trap out."

Biddle listened hard, trying to separate the buzz in his head from the insidious voice. "Five hundred dollars? Too much. If you show it to me, and if I think it's worth it, I'll go two hundred." *What am I saying?* he asked himself. *Pay this greaser money for trapping ground?* But it was said, and he couldn't unsay it.

"You come with me, Lawrence Biddle. I will show you the ground where many beaver work. It is best we go now, for those who claim it may go early to make certain it is untouch. If you are there, your claim clear, then there is nothing they can do. There is no law in these mountains, no deed to the trapping ground, *sí*?"

"Right now?" Biddle thought of something and smiled craftily. "And what if you show me the place and I decide not to pay?"

"I cut your throat," said Morales. "Is most simple."

Biddle felt a sudden chill that almost sobered him. What had he gotten himself into? But he found himself following the Mexican as they gathered their gear from their respective camps and rounded up his packhorses.

They were well on their way toward the pass before the alcohol fumes left his head enough to make him wonder just what had happened. He felt hastily for the reassuring bulk of the belt at his waist, but it was in place. He looked ahead at Morales, who slouched along, his wide hat with its band of conchas slanted down to protect his eyes from the sun.

This was not a reliable man. Was he trying to get his victim away from the other whites in order to rob and kill him? Biddle almost snorted. He was no fool and no weakling. If the bastard tried anything, he'd find himself with his hands full.

Yet as they moved through mountains, across arms of sagebrush flats, and again into mountains, the man made no move against him. As days and nights passed Biddle became sure that this man really knew of the place he described, for he was not moving at random. His route was as direct as the country would allow, and at every point he knew where he was going.

When they climbed into the Absarokas, however, the New Hampshire man was disturbed. This had been one of the first ranges to know the hand of the trapper. Surely it was trapped out even more severely than the rest of the mountains.

Still they climbed, forced at last to lead their mounts as the stony slopes became steeper. They went over a gray ridge, down into a steep valley that held forest and a rushing stream. No lodges, no beaver ponds were there. Up another forbidding ridge and down again into a wider valley they toiled.

At the end of that, where the stream flowed over a lip of rock, they led the horses up a barely passable way formed of wide ledges of stone. At the top they looked down into a place of steams and stinks.

"I can't live down there!" Biddle said as the two stood together in the fetid mists.

"No, no. This is not the place. Not yet. Come still more, and I will show you."

Growing more and more disgruntled, Biddle followed again, but this time when the Mexican paused it was on the edge of a wall-like cliff. Far below, little could be seen because of the thick trees. Only out in the valley was it possible to see the ponds reflecting the sky, the dark dots that were the beaver lodges. This was, indeed, an active beaver stream.

"Looks good. Any more to it?" he asked Morales.

"There's another valley over to the other side, even more hard to get into, but very, very rich. And another lies beyond the fall, up the stream. You will prosper here, amigo. If, that is, you pay me the money you owe for this information."

Biddle, on the off chance that the Mexican could deliver, had stashed two hundred dollars in gold in a pouch slung under his arm. He hauled it out, counted out the coin painfully, as if this was the last he possessed. It never paid to let thieves know that you had money.

"Now you've got my entire poke. If this don't work out, I'll be flat broke, Morales. But it does look good, just like you said. Why you doing this? I really want to know." He wondered for a moment if Morales would answer, though the question was a constant itch.

Then the man sighed and scratched his chin. "A time ago, that *puta* of the gringo Bennett, she shame me before many men. I promise to make the revenge upon them both, and I have done this.

"Down there is the secret place they treasure. When they come here, all happy to think how wise they are to save it for just such time as this, they will find you here, and all their hopes will be destroy."

That made sense to Lawrence Biddle. Revenge was something he understood and approved of. "Sounds like good sense to me. So you go right back to Cuernavaca or wherever and live that good life of yours. I'll dig in here and make the fur fly." He snorted with laughter, and Morales smiled.

Then Biddle thought of something. "How did you get down there? How'd they get their horses down, for that matter? Before you light out, show me the best way to do that."

Without argument, Morales led him along the rim, through tough thickets of young spuce, mountain mahogany, and fir. At last they reached a lower cliff, where a rough slope offered something of an entryway into the valley for those on two feet.

"You can go and come here. But the horse, they must be let down with block and tackle. See the scars on the tree? That is how those two have done this thing. For a price"—he grinned—"I will sell you the block and tackle, which are pack onto my second packhorse. But of course you have no money left. Too bad."

It was highway robbery, but Biddle knew he had to fork

over. Morales, acquired his five hundred after all, leaving Biddle to lower four horses into the valley alone.

Still, Biddle thought as he watched the Mexican move away through the thick growth, he could make enough trapping these remote valleys to make that five hundred look small.

Then he fell to lowering his gear, first of all. He'd leave the horses up here, hobbled so they couldn't go far, until tomorrow, when he'd lower them down without breaking either legs or necks.

It was a good deal. He chuckled as he scrambled down the slope, dropped some twenty feet where it ended, and saw that someone before him had found the perfect camping spot beside a hot spring that breathed steam, not stink, into the crisp air.

He was going to make that fortune, right here where Cleve Bennett had already cleared the way for him. He had nothing against the man, except his stupid choice of a wife. Still, in the world he knew it was dog eat dog, and Biddle was used to doing the eating.

chapter

—7—

Although Cleve was careful not to be obvious about it, he had kept an eye on Julio Morales after he and his new group of henchmen arrived at Rendezvous. He had seen the Mexican do nasty things to people who offended him, since the day when Second Son bested the man.

Cleve knew all too well that some scheme was in the works against his own family. One did not survive for so many years in the mountains without developing a sharp sixth sense about such things. He, too, had dreamed yet again of a buffalo bull, its coat pale with frost, breathing steam into the winter air.

He had asked Prévot and Levreaux to watch the man and Felipe. That was fairly easy for Levreaux to do, for he had to take it easy for some weeks until his wound healed. When Cleve made his way down to the Frenchmen's camp for a spell of talk, he listened with intense interest to Paul's observations.

"He have go away with that Yankee, the Biddle. I do not know what those two may have in common, but anything that take Morales away from here is welcome, I think, *non*?" he said, his wide mouth crinkling into a smile. "You may rest for a time. They take the packhorse and all the supply that Biddle buy with his plew."

"What about Morales?" Cleve asked. "Did he take all his plunder?"

Levreaux thought for a moment. Then he shook his head. "No, he take two packhorse, but he do not take the trap or the winter supply or the stupid Felipe. Those he leave with Carville and those other *canaille*. So he plan to return, it seem clear. Now, why should those two, so different, so unlikely, go away together? It seem ver' queer, *n'est-ce pas*?" He cocked a quizzical brow.

Cleve thought so, too, but he said nothing. This was his annual chance to catch up on news and tall tales and reunions with those of his old companions who still lived. He didn't intend to let this small mystery spoil his holiday. Nevertheless, it was a constant small itch at the back of his mind.

He made the rounds of the trappers' camps and the Indian lodges down in the lower valley, picking up bits of information, new jokes, all sorts of things that would enliven the winter to come. Even those who were closest, like family, sometimes wore hard on each other's nerves as they were cooped up together, enduring the time when the waters froze into iron and one could neither trap nor hunt. New ideas helped to keep tempers under control.

This year there were many different kinds of Indians at Rendezvous. Kiowa, Crow, Pawnee, Oglala and Lakota Sioux, Ute, even Blackfoot had learned to bring furs to the trading meet.

Cleve rambled among the tipis, secure in the knowledge that even those who bore some grudge against him would not risk being banned from future get-togethers in order to make trouble for some old enemy. Though he got some sharp side glances, there was no overt hostility as he made his rounds.

Since his first trip to Rendezvous, he had not aroused really bad blood with any tribe, although the Pawnee still regarded him with cold suspicion. Their young chief, Kills with the Lance, had disappeared that first summer, after taking the vengeance trail against the Bennett family. No sign or trace of him had ever been found.

They would never know the right of it, Cleve thought. Only he and Second Son and Billy-Wolf, then an infant on a cradle board, had been there when Lance made his move and lost. The Pawnee, being wise people, did not start a blood feud simply on suspicion, but he stepped softly around their camp and did not give them any chance to take offense.

However, some of the younger chiefs from other tribes had become his friends. Indeed, this year one of the Cheyenne peace chiefs, Wandering Bear, had brought a group of his Mighty Runner people to the meet. They were not of the clan of Second Son, but they made the Bennetts welcome in their lodges, and Billy-Wolf found welcome playmates among those of his generation among the families in the valley.

Often the family went together to the Mighty Runner camp. There he and his wife sat before the chief's lodge, exchanging gossip and news about the clans now hunting on the plains beyond the mountains. It surprised Cleve that these people now felt more like his own blood kin than his family back in Missouri.

Sometime after his conversation with Levreaux, Cleve was going down to Wandering Bear's camp when he saw Morales sitting at a campfire with the former Yoder group. There was no sign of Lawrence Biddle. Now, where had he gone with the Yankee? The question was troublesome, and it kept bothering him all the way.

When Cleve and his family arrived at the Cheyenne camp, he hunkered down, as he had learned to do over the years, and watched for a chance to question his host. The Cheyenne did not sit quietly in camp for long; the younger hunters had been out ranging these mountains into which their people seldom came.

Perhaps one of those had seen the Mexican returning from his trek with the New Hampshire man. That would satisfy Cleve's curiosity, if nothing else.

When the pipe had been passed and the older warriors were talking quietly, Cleve leaned toward Wandering Bear. "Morales is back. I wonder if any of your young hunters might have seen him as he returned. The direction he came from interests me. I do not trust him, you understand, and I like to keep an eye on his comings and goings." Speaking the guttural Cheyenne felt as natural to him now as his native English or the Latin that his mother had taught him in his childhood.

Bear's bronze face remained smooth, but one brow quirked very slightly. "My nephew Otter Foot was stalking an elk when the man came down the trail from the pass to the north. Alone, with two packhorses. Is that helpful?"

Cleve grunted his thanks, but he found himself feeling a chill of foreboding. If he could watch Morales, then surely Morales could watch him. Why had he not thought of that? But he managed to remain calm and polite as he took his leave of the Mighty Runners clan and moved toward his own lodge with his family.

As soon as Billy-Wolf was settled for the night, Cleve beckoned Ferris and Second Son to the fire outside the tipi. "I think we need to pack up and skedaddle," he said, gazing into the fire as he poked it with a dry branch.

"I have a bad feeling. The sooner we get to our trapping ground, the better I'll feel about things. Could be—could be that Mexican spied it out by following us last summer and has showed it to that damn Biddle."

Second Son's eyes widened, then narrowed, and he knew she was examining his thought and finding it bitter. There was, however, only one way to learn if his guess was accurate.

"I might as well make it back home," said Ferris. "You're going the opposite of my direction. But if you need me, just get word to me. I'll pull these old bones out of my house for the younker in there. You two kin take care of yourselves, without any need of a codger like me." He grinned, and Cleve understood that the old man would die for any one of them, whatever he might say.

They rolled into their sleeping skins, and soon the lodge

was filled with the quiet breathing of Second Son and the boy, as well as the rasping snores of Joe Ferris. But Cleve found it hard to sleep.

Why had he not foreseen this possibility? He chided himself for borrowing trouble. It might all be in his imagination, with Biddle moving well off into another range of mountains entirely. Morales was sneaky enough to cheat even a New Hampshire man, Bennett thought. Biddle hadn't struck him as any too bright, when he talked with him.

When he woke, he lay for a moment staring up into the dim cone that was the top of the tipi. The sound of crackling outside told him that his wife and Ferris were already up, the fire built, and the iron coffeepot already set into the coals to boil. He could smell the first wisps of fragrant steam as he rolled out of his furs and pulled on his moccasins.

Cleve was distracted as he ate a handful of dried meat and drank his coffee. His mind was far up the Absarokas, dreading what he might find when his family reached the cliff overlooking their valley.

Ferris rode away early on his homeward journey. Once he had hugged them all and tossed Billy-Wolf high, despite the boy's gangling length, he mounted his old mare and did not look back. Looking back was a bad idea for anyone living among the mountains. It led to thoughts of old friends lost and new friends that one might never see again. Cleve understood the old man's attitude.

When his own family pulled out, leading their string of horses, he waved at Emile Prévot and Paul Levreaux, who were standing beside the trading shed, talking with a couple of latecomers. They raised their hands, their faces solemn. They, too, understood the terrible uncertainties that accompanied those who left their friends. Like them, Cleve passed on and did not look back.

Second Son took the lead, as usual, followed by the packhorses. Billy-Wolf, riding Blaze, rode in the middle of the pack string, keeping the horses from straying off the path.

Cleve was mounted on another Socks, a good-sized stallion he'd traded for after his old Socks grew too old for hard riding. He was shaping up well, Bennett thought, and promised to be worthy of his name.

Now the old Socks ran free on the plain with the Cheyenne herd. Cleve was teaching this new animal the skills that had saved his life in the old days when the obedience of his horse meant survival. He seemed to learn quickly, and already he responded to whistles.

They rode away northward toward the pass that would take them over into the Wind River country. Beyond that rose the gray line of the Shadow Mountains, which the white men called the Absarokas. It took them days of travel to reach the stream leading up into the heights from which they could make their way to their old trapping ground.

As they neared their goal Cleve felt his heart rise. There he had lived with his wife and Holy William. There his son had been born. There he had bound his old enemy, Jules Terrebonne, to a tree and left him to stand guard forever over the grave of the skinny preacher who had saved the lives of all the Bennetts and died for it.

But a dark shadow seemed to move on the heights, following the clouds and his own foreboding. As they went up into the forests and beyond, he often looked into the eyes of his wife when they stopped to rest the horses. He saw reflected there his own dismay at the thought of what they might find when they came to the end of their journey.

They climbed the rough ledges of stone to the ridge edging the first valley, where the stink of sulfur was as terrible as ever. They camped in the forest beyond the fogs of steam, and they built no fire. By common consent, the three of them huddled together and murmured over their meal of jerky.

"We will come to the cliff tomorrow," Cleve said softly. "I fear what we may find."

Second Son, her eyes dark in the dimming light, said, "We will find someone there. I saw three hoofmarked stones as we came up the slope. Two bent-stem leaves hung above the path. Someone has come this way before us."

Cleve had been watching, but so faint had been those traces that he had missed them. He would, he knew, never develop the keen eye that his wife's Cheyenne upbringing had given her. Too often, her survival had depended upon noticing just such subtle marks.

He sighed. Should they turn now without learning what lay ahead? But he knew he could never do that.

If Biddle was there, they must challenge him, though by all the unspoken rules of trapping, the man on the ground had the rights there for the season. It was a sad thing, losing something that had been indisputably yours. But it would be worse to go away without trying to reason with the man who had followed Morales here.

With first light they were up. Second Son tied their horses to trees well before they reached the cliff overlooking the valley, and the three crept to the edge and looked over.

A light wind made the spruces whisper above their heads, and on that wind rode a faint scent of smoke. Cleve's heart sank. There was, indeed, someone down there in the place they had felt was solely and securely their own.

He wondered if there was any way to convince Biddle of their prior claim. Or would documented proof be of any benefit at all? He had judged the Yankee to be one of the hardheaded breed that salted sugar and watered milk.

It was doubtful if he had any reason or honor to appeal to.

chapter

—8—

Lawrence Biddle hummed as he puttered about his campsite, cutting back brush that had grown into the clearing the Bennetts had made for their earlier campsite. He had found the hot spring, too, and it tempted him with thoughts of a steaming bath.

He had never been one who was particular about washing himself, but he had indulged in a hot bath just once, when he came through St. Louis. He recalled that long soak with much pleasure, and this one would be free!

He sniffed at the shoulder of his greasy shirt. If a tomcat had pissed on him, it wouldn't smell much different. There couldn't be more privacy anywhere than there was here in this hidden valley; he could spare the time to soak himself as long as he wanted, if he shriveled up like a prune doing it.

He had checked the beaver ponds in the next two valleys and found them fat with busy animals, nibbling down aspen and willow and storing them near their lodges, secured in their dams. Until frost made the fur thicken and gleam, there wasn't much to do. He would, by damn, take him a bath.

He stripped off the woolen shirt and put it to soak in a downstream pool that bubbled gently as a washpot. The water turned black and started to stink, sending a dark trickle down into the stony runnel below it. Biddle grunted and pulled off his pants, which joined the shirt.

His long johns were another matter. He had to sit on a stump and cut the stitches that had secured them since last fall. They peeled away at last with a rush of odor that shocked even him, leaving him staring down at his pale hide. It was dotted with reddish freckles and streaked with dirt. He'd rolled down slopes and been pitched off horses and sweated a whole hell of a lot since last he tended to his own skin.

Bare as a new-pulled radish, and about as dirty, he rummaged through his plunder to find the scrap of lye soap he'd tucked away. Then, holding it high, he stepped into the steaming water and sank slowly into its depths.

There was a rock just right for sitting on with his head above water. He put the soap by for future reference and sighed. His skin itched frantically for a while, but then he began to relax, leaning back against the boulder at the edge of the pool.

He sighed with pleasure. In a bit he'd scrub, but for the moment he was just going to rest and enjoy.

As the heat penetrated his muscles he became drowsy. Slowly his head settled back against the boulder on which he had placed the soap; his arms floated to the top of the water, keeping him from slipping sideways.

He dreamed of St. Louis: the bathhouse where he had dolled up and the brothel where he had spent more than he intended on painted women and watered liquor. A smile stretched his lips, and he let himself drift into those pleasurable memories.

How long he slept he never knew. He woke, however, with the instant realization that something was very wrong. The bird that had been squawking overhead had gone silent, which was probably what woke him, and he felt eyes looking at him.

He opened his own eyes a slit and examined the patch of grass and bushes within eyeshot. There he had entered the pool, for the other banks were steep and slippery.

Instead of being empty except for his rifle and knife belt, he saw there a short, stocky Indian dressed in a hide shirt and leggings; the Indian was looking at Biddle with what might have been disgust, if he'd let expression show on his face.

Biddle sat upright, forgetting the slickness of the rock. Down he went, head and all.

Before Biddle could manage to get his legs under him, a hard hand caught his arm and he shot upward through the water. His feet scrabbled at the slick bottom of the pool until they found purchase and let him stand.

"Who the hell are you?" he sputtered. He began wading toward the low bank. He had to dress himself—and then he thought with horror that all his clothing was bubbling in that pool, which was some ten yards from his present location. It might be better to stay where he was until he knew what was going on.

His rescuer was wading out of the water, which had come much higher on him than on the tall, lanky Biddle. As the dark-skinned warrior climbed out, the deerskin clung to his body, and it came to the New Hampshire man that this was not the shape of any warrior he'd ever seen. When the Indian turned, Biddle recognized Bennett's Cheyenne wife.

If he hadn't already been scarlet from the heat of the pool, he'd have blushed all over; however, as things stood, there was no way to tell. He sank instantly, chest-deep.

Damn! Here he was, exposed to a woman, even if she was an Indian, without his weapons, and about as helpless as a man can be. Being naked under those circumstances was the most frightening thing he'd ever faced.

He made a private resolve never again to remove all his clothing at once and probably never to indulge in another bath as long as he lived. If he died among Christians, they'd wash him. If not, it made no difference anyway; he'd stink worse before he was done.

"You're the Bennett woman." That wasn't the smartest thing he'd ever said, but never before had he confronted a woman at such a disadvantage.

"I am Second Son," she said. "And you are in our place. We put our mark on this valley long ago. Look at the tree!" She pointed to the big aspen that leaned over the pool.

There, sure enough, he saw that the bark had been carved with a circle enclosing a deep *B.* But that didn't mean a thing, he knew. There was no law here, no claim to land, no way to enforce such a claim if there had been.

"You just go and let me be for a bit while I get something on, and we'll talk about it," he said. If he could gain some time, get to his weapons, he'd run that red-tail woman and her family out of here. He'd paid good money for this trapping ground.

She nodded, turned, and bent to pick up his rifle and the knife belt before stalking away among the thick-growing young spruces.

"DAMMITTOHELL!" he yelled. But that didn't even bring a laugh from her. Grumbling under his breath, Biddle climbed out of the pool and moved down to the place where he had left his washing. The wool was heavy and sodden, but it had boiled cleaner. The long johns were pink instead of dark brown, too. He heaved them out and pulled them on, though they stuck to him, resisting all the way.

Putting the wool shirt on was miserable, for it stuck to his underwear as well as to his hide. The pants went on, too, and he stood barefoot, with streams of brownish water running down his legs and puddling on the ground at his feet.

Never in all his proper New England life had Lawrence Biddle been in such a fix. Wet as a beaver, his weapons in the hands of the woman he had knowingly displaced from her rightful ground, he knew that he was helpless. That bastard Bennett was probably lurking around someplace, too, waiting for an excuse to part his hair with one of those arrows he could place so accurately when they had a shooting match at Rendezvous.

Muttering curses, he tried to dry his feet enough to slip on his moccasins, but the drips from his wet clothing kept trickling into them, making them squish at every step. As he moved out of the thicket fringing the pool, he saw the woman and her son waiting at his camp.

If he hadn't heard the tales about how she beat the tar out of Morales, he might have jumped her, disregarding the boy entirely. But he had listened while the trappers talked, these past two summers, and it was possible that even the child of these unorthodox people might prove dangerous. He swallowed hard and decided not to risk it.

"Bennett!" he called. "Show yourself!"

There was the faintest whisper of sound—a hide shirt brushing through spruce branches, perhaps—and a voice said, "Right behind you, Biddle. You just go on ahead and make yourself comfortable. I think Second Son's built up your fire so you can dry off. You look mighty wet to me."

So Bennett had been right there at the pool all the time, without giving any sign of his presence. Again Biddle swallowed. These were hard people, dangerous and tough, and he knew he'd better use every bit of his New England salesmanship to keep them from killing him and taking back their trapping grounds.

The boy had brought dry wood from someplace; probably they had left their own stash of firewood the last time they visited the place. The flames climbed the pyramid of sticks, and he backed up to the warmth gratefully. At these heights, even in summer it was always chilly.

Cleve Bennett hunkered down on the other side of the fire, and his wife and son withdrew into the spruces, about some business of their own. "You didn't find this place yourself, did you?" the blond trapper asked.

Biddle shook his head, his wet hair flapping about his neck. "No, I didn't. That Mex Morales come up to me and offered to sell me the location of some untouched trapping country. I'd of been a fool to turn him down."

Bennett stared into the coals, twiddling a twig between his callused fingers. "I see your point," he said, and Biddle's heart began to rise out of his mocassins.

"But you knew when you made that deal that he was getting revenge against my wife, didn't you?"

This man got right to the point without pussyfooting around, that was clear. Not much room to wiggle, Biddle thought.

A wildly unorthodox idea came to him. It was something that would have made his grandfather rise up in his grave, if it had ever been suggested to him. But with this particular set of people, it seemed the only way to go: he was going to tell the whole, plain truth.

"Let me tell you my problem," Biddle began, squatting and holding his hands toward the fire. "I'm kind of between a rock and a hard place, Mr. Bennett. This was my last chance to make it out here, else I have to go back to New Hampshire."

Bennett looked up. "Why?" He really seemed interested, and his tone was not hostile.

Reassured, Biddle recalled the circumstances that had brought him out here into this wild and desolate country. He didn't really like it, and that was something he hadn't faced before.

"My grandpa built a good business back in Biddleton. Started a hardware store with money he inherited from his kin back in the old country. With people farming and starting blacksmith and carpentry and other kinds of businesses, he had more demand for tools and other equipment than he could meet, but he kept making deals with ship captains to bring in orders from manufacturers in England, and he made it big."

Bennett nodded. "Sounds like a smart man."

"My father was smart, too. Kept that business growing, and me and my brother grew right up with it and in it, so to speak. I knew how to heft nails and give the proper weight without a scale before I was waist-high. I loved that business, lived, breathed, almost ate it for breakfast, all the time I was coming up.

"My brother didn't. He liked the money, but he hated the work, the tools, even the customers. But he"—Biddle sighed—"was the oldest by two years. He was willed the business when Pa died, and I got a fair amount of cash. Just the opposite from what it ought to be."

"Why didn't you offer to buy the business with the money you inherited?" asked Bennett.

"Think I'm a fool? 'Course I did that, first thing. But Elliott had always wanted me under his thumb. He wanted a lot more than I inherited for the store, but he made me an offer. I could *run* the business for him. Let him lie back and loaf while I sweated for a wage you wouldn't offer a freedman to haul manure. I turned him down flat.

"Came out here to see if I couldn't parlay the money I had into enough to buy him out. But I hit the mountains too late. Other folks had skimmed off the cream with trading, and the beaver streams were running dry.

"If I go back with my tail between my legs, Elliott'll

never let me forget it. I just can't do that, Mr. Bennett. It sticks in my craw."

The pale eyes glanced up at him, bright in the light of fire and sun reflected from the eastern cliff. To Biddle's surprise, the man looked sympathetic.

"You know, I understand how you feel. I had problems with my own family back when I was younger, and it took years before I could go back and see them again. This place means a lot to you, doesn't it?"

To his dismay, Biddle felt tears form at the corners of his eyes. He hadn't known until right now how very much it did mean, for he hadn't put everything into words before. Wordless, he nodded.

"Then I guess I'll talk to Second Son and see if she agrees to go another direction. You wait here, Mr. Biddle. I'll be back in a bit." The trapper rose, his big body solid in the clear light, and turned silently into the spruces.

Biddle sat beside the fire, his clothing steaming, his mind in a turmoil. This was what simple honesty could do? By damn, he had to remember that if he ever got back to New Hampshire and bought the business back!

chapter 9

Second Son had recognized a restlessness in her mate for the past two winters. In summer, with Rendezvous and travel and other distractions, he seemed quite happy. Yet when they settled into their chosen trapping place, built their shelter, and distributed their traps in the ponds and pools of the area, he seemed different. Not unhappy, exactly; he gave her the same feeling she had known when watching a colt tethered to a stake or a puppy tied beside a tipi.

He and Billy-Wolf often hunted together while she

tended the traps. That was fine with her, for she knew that only through tiring himself thoroughly would he be able to survive the long weeks of deep snow.

This year she had dreaded the coming autumn. All the time she was at Rendezvous she had kept her sharp ears tuned to the conversations taking place around her and had seen Cleve's eyes light up when he spoke with Prévot and Levreaux about Malachi Walters's expedition to the coast. He wanted to be one of that group, she knew.

She had wondered, when they set out to learn if Morales had betrayed the location of their trapping valley, if this would be the excuse Cleve needed to turn aside from the increasingly discouraging life that trapping had become. She had hoped as much, for her people did not bind themselves to such demanding tasks unless they were necessary for their survival.

When Cleve emerged from the spruces to find her sitting with Billy-Wolf on a ledge of rock against the cliff, she saw at once that he had news. His expression was animated, and his eyes blazed with enthusiasm.

"I think we've just lucked out," he said, dropping onto the ledge beside her. "This man Biddle is in a bind, and he needs a good trapping year mighty bad. With things like they are, if he brings in a good catch, he should get enough to do what he wants.

"On the other hand, we've got more gold than is good for us stashed in that bear den up yonder in the heights. Would you be disappointed if we didn't trap for a while?"

She looked down at Billy-Wolf. He grinned up at her, his white-eye blood revealed strongly. Sometimes he was all Cheyenne, his face under complete control. This time she could see that he, too, would like to do something different. Something interesting, involving other people.

"My people do not live like this," she said quietly. "We like to be free to ride away, if it seems a good thing to do. We like to see new country, meet others from distant places, when there is the opportunity. I do not object, if you want to leave Biddle here. We enjoyed this place when we were young, but now we are older. I, too, would like to see the Great Water that the white men speak about."

"Me, too!" shrilled Billy-Wolf. "I want to see it, too."

Cleve's grin was wider than the boy's. "Then we'll go back and meet Walters. He's going to be at Rendezvous for a while yet, getting men for his group." His grin faded, and he looked very uncomfortable.

"But I'm afraid the boy isn't old enough for such a rough trip. I talked to some of Smith's people who went with him to the coast, and it's a mighty hard deal. I think he ought to go back to live with Singing Wolf while we go west."

Second Son could feel her son's disappointment; she touched him comfortingly. He had wilted like a broken-stem leaf, and she felt sudden pain on his behalf.

Yet disappointment was a part of life, and those who could not deal with it did not survive. This would be a stern lesson that he needed, for he had lived, so far, under the shelter of his parents' concern. They had, she often thought, made his life too easy.

"A time with your uncle will be good training for you," she said. "Your brother Lightning will take you on hunts, and you will ride with other young warriors on small raids.

This is a thing that you need to learn, as I did, before you become a man."

The small dark face beneath the startling light brown hair brightened. "You think he will let me?" he asked. "And I will see old Socks. I can ride Blaze with the other boys. I think I will like that."

She glanced back at Cleve, who was grinning again with relief. If there was any flaw in him, it was his reluctance to disappoint their son.

They camped that night in the familiar valley, some distance from their old spot where Biddle had set up his own camp. Second Son found herself breathing deeply, savoring the fresh scent of the firs and spruces, the lung-piercing cleanliness of the mountain air. How long might it be before she came here again?

Would she *ever* come here again? She had listened as the trappers talked of the Smith expedition to the Great Water. That had been a terrible journey, and many men and more horses had died along the way. She knew, as all her people did, that life was fragile and temporary.

Anyone could die at any time, in this world of plains and mountains and wild creatures. On such a long trek, it was possible that this group would suffer as that other had. Still, if one lived, one must take risks, that was the rule of this land. Life without danger was flavorless and dull and without value.

Lying in her blanket roll, staring up through a net of spruce tips at a black sky studded with brilliant stars, she thought of new places, people of a kind she had never known, dangers she had not yet encountered. Her heart beat faster, anticipating the challenge such things would bring.

Her brother had taught her well, when she was a very young warrior, riding on her first raid with the boys of the clan. . . .

She recalled that morning, the air as clean as this, the world just turning from gray to pink as the sun rose. There had been six of them, all of an age to begin their lives as warriors, and this was a daring dawn raid on the horses of a nearby Pawnee village.

Singing Wolf, being older and having several raids behind him, did not ride with them. Instead he remained behind, watching, as Two Bears, the oldest of the youngsters, kicked his horse into a gallop and waved his coup stick above his head.

She could still feel the devouring excitement of that ride, the grass whipping past her bare knees, the smell of horse and smoke and dust mingled in her small nose. Her heart had pounded to match the pounding hooves as they rode.

They had driven away a dozen horses from the herd, whose sleepy watchman had waked to four coup sticks bounding off him in quick succession. He had ridden after them, his yells shrill on the morning air, but they had returned to the Burning Hearts triumphant. She had ridden in as fourth, and it had earned her her first eagle feather.

She had earned her first two horses in that foray as well, for they had been shared out among the successful raiders. No longer was she a "boy," riding her father's horses. Now she had her own, as well as a place—well back—in the circle of men around the fire.

She had not noticed or cared that the girls in the village giggled behind their hands when she passed—who paid attention to girls, anyway? No warrior wasted his time with such things.

A few years later she learned to her chagrin that the other warriors did not go by her rules. They glanced sideways at giggling girls, even made excuses to visit the stream at the time when the youngest women went there with pitch-lined baskets or waterskins.

Disgusted, Second Son had devoted all her time and her energies to becoming the best rider, the best bowman, the best horse stealer and raider in the village. In her own age group, she succeeded, but she had felt that nothing would do until she could equal her older brother, Singing Wolf.

She sighed and rolled closer to Cleve, listening to the long cry of a wolf on some neighboring height. A message from her brother? Possibly. He had sent his totemic beast to sing on the height on the night when Billy-Wolf was born.

She thought with pleasure of going with her son back to the Burning Heart village, wherever it might be this summer. She would, as usual, build a fire on some high place and lay on damp fuel until it smoked, then use a blanket to signal. That would bring her brother to find her, and together they would take her son back to her people.

This was a good thing, she felt, burrowing her nose into Cleve's back. Her son needed to learn the ways of his people without the presence of his parents. Cleve was a passable Cheyenne, but he still had difficulty with some of their customs. He objected to stealing horses, though he seemed to have no problem with having someone steal their valley. But who understood the ways of white men?

• • •

She woke before the sky paled and rolled quietly out of the blankets. Cleve snorted but did not wake as she donned her moccasins and robe and stole away through the spruces. They would leave early, and before going, she wanted to climb fast and look down into that other valley past the western ridge, where the bones of Holy William lay, guarded by those of Jules Terrebonne.

To look upon the dead was not a thing her people did, but she had memories of that place that time had not erased. Her son was born there, beneath a spruce tree, and from that height her brother's totem beast had sung to the stars. Something deep inside her needed a last glimpse into the past, though she felt strange about that need.

Perhaps she had lived with a white man too long, learning from him ways that were alien to her own kind. As she climbed she thought of that, but once she came to the top of the difficult cliff, she forgot her concern.

The valley was brimming with mist, rising from the hot springs into the chill air of the heights. She could glimpse between drifts of steam the pale reflection of water and the darker dots that were beaver lodges.

A song rose in her heart; she drew a deep breath and began to sing a quiet, quavering chant of farewell to the past and welcome to the unknown future. Beyond the valley, a wolf howled in reply.

Drumming gently with one finger against the leather of her robe, she sang on, knowing that in the shape of that wolf her brother had greeted her. Today she would ride east to take her son home to the Burning Hearts, while

Cleve rode south and west to speak for a place in Walters's expedition.

Singing Wolf would be watching for her signal. The thought warmed her as she turned back toward the camp and the beginning of that new journey.

chapter

—10—

Although Cleve had spent very little time apart from his family since he and Second Son married, he rode away from the Absarokas with a light heart. He had lived until he was nineteen as his father's slave on the Missouri farm.

Then, instead of being freed from such labor in this new life, he had found trapping to be equally demanding. Though it had been his own free choice, still it had been a new kind of slavery, this time to his own purposes.

Used to that as he was, he had grown weary of doing the same kind of thing, winter after winter. When he thought about it, he understood that his wife felt the same. Her people, as she had told him, did not harness themselves to such matters but rode free over the plains and the mountains, surviving with difficulty sometimes but uninterested in putting together great piles of possessions.

Warned by the ambush of the earlier group heading for Rendezvous, Cleve did not take the main pass back toward the river, but climbed higher, leading Socks in order to reach the top of the far steeper game trail that wandered along the high slopes. So it was that he came down toward the river from an unexpected direction and saw below him two men, crouched behind boulders, watching the only trail usable by loaded horses, which led toward the lowland along the river.

He ground-hitched Socks and crept along just below the ridge on which he had stood, keeping an eye on the pair. He had a gut feeling that there would be more of them, probably waiting for someone who had sold his plews for gold and was heading back to Missouri to blow his gains on a major fling. Or even, he thought with some degree of surprise, to bushwhack one of the traders, loaded with a year's worth of beaver and lynx and marten and wolverine furs.

He found a spur of rock that concealed him from below while affording him a good view of the windings of the trail leading down to the Green. He spotted from that point another man on the cliff beyond the track. He seemed to be hunkered down, his rifle across the stone on which he leaned.

When he tipped back his fur hat and stared down at the trail, Cleve recognized Felipe, Morales's stupid companion.

He had indeed run onto a well-laid ambush, intended,

Cleve had no doubt, to send its leaders away with a lot of unearned loot. He looked hard toward the most distant visible part of the trail, but as yet only the tiny shape of the first traveler could be seen coming into view around a wooded angle.

That meant that he had time for a little surprise of his own, he thought. By God, he felt nineteen again, full of gin and vinegar, ready to tackle a bear and give it the first two bites. He slid backward out of sight and then ran to where he'd left Socks.

There was a runnel that drained the height above him, and Cleve led the horse carefully down the zigzag route, avoiding tumbles of loose rock that might go clattering down and warn his intended victims of his approach. A ledge of stone ran away at a slant, promising to intersect the trail some distance above the bandits' position, and he followed it, glad that it was wide enough for his horse's belly to clear the cliff behind it.

They came out on a stone apron an easy leap above the path. Socks, already trained to obey even the most obviously insane demand from his master, sprang down, landing with a rattle of hooves on rock. Cleve dropped onto his back and kicked him in the flanks.

"Ho, boy!" he urged the stallion, and the mettlesome horse turned to gallop down the trail toward the waiting men.

It is highly dangerous to gallop a horse down a steep slope. Its fragile legs may break if it hits an unexpected hole or ditch; in that case its rider goes over its head onto his own, which can be as fragile as the animal's leg bones. Many a man had died, Cleve knew, from using just such foolhardy tactics.

But he was nineteen again, just for the moment, immortal and willing to dare anything. As he dashed around a dogleg bend in the track, Cleve saw startled faces appear above their concealing bushes and boulders.

"HI-EEEEEEE-YO!" he yelled, kicking Socks again. He fitted an arrow to his bow, knowing that what he was going to try would not work with a flintlock.

"You up ahead! There's thieves waiting for you. Take care!"

He couldn't see anyone except the pair of bushwhackers he had spotted earlier; those two now rose to take aim at him. Using the trick he'd learned from Singing Wolf, Cleve dropped on one side of Socks, holding by a foot secured in a leather loop as he took quick aim and loosed an arrow at the bandit on that side of the trail.

The man dropped, and Cleve knew he had hit him, whether fatally or not it was impossible to tell. He pulled himself back astride and nocked another arrow, which he let fly at the other bushwhacker, who was in the act of ducking into the bushes.

Then Socks was past, flying down the crooked track amid a clatter of rocks and hoofbeats. "Take cover!" Cleve yelled as he rounded a series of sharp angles and came out on the straight segment at the end of which he had seen the traveler coming.

He rode pell-mell after those who had cleared the forest-hidden part of the trail before his warning. Once everyone was under cover, he pulled up his sweating mount and slung his bow over his shoulder again.

"Whoooeee!" he grunted. "I'm getting too old for such things."

"Cleve Bennett!" said a familiar voice. "I think you are

the fool, *oui*? To ride the horse down that incline, it is the ultimate in crazy." Emile Prévot dismounted and waved to his companions to do the same.

"You say the bandit is there on the trail?"

"Well, I saw three, all hidden, all with guns, all waiting for something. I felt as if you didn't want to find out what that might be," Cleve said, dropping from the horse to clap Prévot on the back. "I don't like to see friends get shot up if I can help it."

Already, four of Prévot's companions were climbing the slope in the cover of brush and boulders. In time they would come up on the place where the ambushers had hidden, and then they would either bring back bodies or they would find traces of those who had waited there.

"I did not think to see you again so soon," said Prévot. He fumbled behind his saddle and brought out a water-skin. "You would like the drink while we wait? It will be some time before we know what happen up there, I think."

"You always were a liar," Cleve commented as a combination of yells and shots shattered the quiet. "Sounds as if your boys found more than I saw up there. Why don't we mosey upward and see what we can do to help?"

Leaving two of the party to guard horses and supplies, Prévot motioned the rest to flank the trail. "Take care, *mes amis*," he said. "Those are the animal there, and they have no honor. I will go alone up the trail, on foot, to draw the fire."

"And I'll be right beside you," Cleve said, his tone too firm to allow argument.

Emile nodded, his eyes busy checking every shadow

under a rock or twitch amid the greenery. Together the two started upward, and a long hot trek it was on foot.

Above them occasional shots told them that some of the bandits had holed up and were holding off the scouts. Cleve's educated ear had learned to detect things he had never known as a youngster in Missouri: he heard a death rattle off in the rubble beyond the track, and he hoped it was not one of their own people.

He could tell the difference between the different Hawkens and a very old Henry. Someone was moaning softly, and someone else was cursing quietly but with great inventiveness.

"Ssss!" he hissed.

Emile turned, and Cleve gestured toward a runnel that gave access to the higher ground without being quite so exposed. The Frenchman nodded, and they moved up the rough streambed, their moccasins feeling a way among the water-rounded rocks.

Beyond a thicket of mountain mahogany they found the first wounded man, lying on his side as if to hold himself together. He was the source of those moans.

Cleve bent over, knife in hand in case of treachery, but he saw at once that this one was not going to live. He'd been gut-shot, and his face was already livid.

"Porter," he whispered to Prévot. "Rode with Carville. I'll take care of him." He slit the man's throat quickly, and they moved on before the body stopped twitching.

They came out on a bluff overlooking the trail below. Two men were running desperately from the scene of battle, pursued by several of Prévot's people.

That bluff had been the position of the man he'd shot with his first arrow, Cleve thought. Even as he peered down through the tangled bushes, Prévot touched his shoulder.

"There," the Frenchman said. "Under the big rock—and that is an arrow I see. You have shoot this one, eh?"

It was Felipe, the henchman of Morales. He was quite dead. They found three others as well, after hailing Prévot's men and calling them in. Morales, however, was nowhere in sight.

Once they had things sorted out, the horses led up, and Prévot's party ready to go on, Cleve looked up at the old man and asked, "Is Walters still down on the Green? Second Son and I decided we want to go with him. Morales sold us out to that Yankee Biddle, but we're about tired of trapping, anyway."

"He have find almost enough men, but still he wait for more. If you hurry, you may find him still in camp. *Bonne chance, mon ami.*" Emile kicked his horse into motion and turned up the steep trail.

Cleve stood aside and watched them go; a few were men he had known for years; some of them he had just met, but he knew that many would never meet him again this side of the grave. Then he strode back down to Socks and mounted the stallion.

"Let's go, boy," he said. "We're about to take us a *trip*."

chapter 11

Malachi Walters sat on a stump, warming his feet at a small fire. Behind him there was a flurry of activity as the last of his recruits took a final chugalug from a jug of whiskey or rummaged about making certain that nothing had been forgotten.

Several of the younger members of the trapping fraternity were making for the east again, discouraged with the poor harvests of the past couple of years. The older men, spoiled to the freedom of the life they had found here in the wild country, were drifting away toward whatever goals they had chosen. Malachi hated to see Prévot go, with Levreaux, but both had felt unable to accompany his expedition.

He was disappointed that so few of those old hands had chosen to go west with him. There, he felt sure, he and Beeville would find rich trapping and hunting again. In time, most of these men who were giving up would have found new opportunities in California.

He sighed and held the other moccasined foot close to the coals. It was warm on the coast, he'd heard, and that would be a welcome thing. He got colder the older he became.

There was a call in the distance, and he looked up. Someone was riding up to hitch beside the remnant of the trading shed. The sun glanced off a fur cap and a swatch of bright blond hair—Bennett? Was that Cleve Bennett returning?

Walters rose hurriedly and headed down toward the shed, where the big man was talking with one of the lingering Indians. Sun Turns Red was only now getting ready to return to his people's hunting grounds. That morning he had made the rounds of the remaining camps, cadging whiskey at every stop. By now the old fellow was beginning to walk with careful dignity, his feathered hat cocked at a rakish angle.

"Bennett! What are you doing back here?" Walters called.

The tall trapper and the shorter Indian turned. Cleve grinned as he came toward Malachi, his hand out.

"I came back to see if you still want us to come with you to California," he said. "We found somebody in our old trapping spot, and we decided that we've just about trapped ourselves to death. Time we saw some more of the country. You still need men?"

Walters allowed himself a wide grin. He had wanted Bennett for his intelligence and ability to plan; he had wanted his wife because she was a skilled tracker, a fierce warrior, and as an Indian she could probably help to communicate with other tribes they would meet along the way.

For an instant he wondered what the more traditional Indian wives of some of the other men would make of her. Then he discarded the thought. Whatever they thought—or did—Second Son could take care of it. He had heard the tales of her encounters with randy mountain men who thought her a woman for the taking, like the young women for sale among the tipis.

"I still have room, and I'm surely glad to see you. I had hoped Prévot and Levreaux would come, but those two claimed to be too old for such a hard trip. I'd rather have one of them than ten of the kind of newcomer we're getting out here these days. They seem to quit whenever things get a little rough."

Cleve grunted his agreement. "I met Emile up toward the pass," he said. "He was about to be bushwhacked, but I managed to warn him and we busted it up. Is Morales still here? Or Carville?"

The connection was obvious, though Walters felt a bit surprised that bandits would strike so close to the Rendezvous site. "I saw Morales head out this morning with about a dozen men. Carville left last night."

He rubbed his chin, thinking hard. "I wondered if they split up—that'd be the shortest partnership in history, if they did. You think it was them tried to ambush Prévot?"

"Morales's dumb friend Felipe was killed up there. A

couple more looked like men who rode with Carville. I'll bet they split up for their own purposes and sent some to steal what they could. Then it's likely that the two bunches intended to join up later," Bennett said.

Walters nodded. "Bad bunch, there. I wondered when Morales rode in with them if it wasn't a sign of trouble to come. I'm glad I'm heading out. Yoder was pretty stupid, but that Mexican is shrewd and sneaky and altogether bad news."

He stared past Bennett, looking for the packhorses and Second Son. "Where's your wife?"

"She's gone to take the boy to her brother's folks," he said. "She'll meet us along the way—you couldn't hide from her any way you tried. She knows Socks's track as well as she knows mine."

Bennett glanced back toward the forested slope behind him. "I left the packhorses back yonder in the shade, still loaded, in case you intend to pull out today. If you don't, I'll go bring them in and unload."

"We go today. The men are getting ready right now. We should be leaving in just a little bit. Then Sun Turns Red can go home . . . all the whiskey'll be gone." Walters smiled at the old chief, who grinned back, his face a map of wrinkles.

It was a bit longer than that, but at last Walters headed south between the two mountain ranges. He intended to cross by way of a pass he'd found earlier, then head back west over the gentler Wasatch Range. Going north of the Great Salt Lake should take his group through easier country than Jed Smith had found farther to the south.

It was late August by then, but two cloudbursts and a

snowstorm surprised them along the way. That didn't slow them down much, however. On the fifth day after Walters rode away from the Green, Cleve Bennett's wife caught up with the file of men.

She rode quietly up beside her husband, without saying a word, and Walters asked no questions. Altogether, she was a surprising woman. If she was here, all was well with her son and her family, and he didn't need to ask about them.

Before they reached the Wasatch crossing, which led down into the valley of the Great Salt Lake at its northern end, Walters found Beeville waiting for him with several more experienced mountain men.

This brought the tally of the expedition's forces to some fifty seasoned white men, some dozen of whom had brought with them squaws they had obtained from different tribes. In addition, he had bought, bartered for, and otherwise obtained a sizable herd of extra horses, for he was a great believer in having more mounts than you needed. More than once, that tendency of his had saved his neck.

There were, in addition, three Indian scouts: a Ute, a Pawnee, and a Yaqui who had come from the southern deserts and should be of great help in the desert portions of their journey. All were silent men, whose wives kept to themselves, as if contemptuous of those women who had paired with white men.

They rested the horses, redistributed the supplies among the pack animals, and mapped their proposed route as they rested beside Bear River, before tackling the Wasatch crossing. Beeville kept in the background, letting Malachi choose routes and lead his men, which was a great help.

Most of the group had come only because it was Walters who asked them and they trusted his judgment.

The valley of the Bear was a pleasant place, sheltered by ranges along both sides, with wide meadows full of game. The lake, blue and clean and clear, provided abundant water. The grass was lush, and Walters made sure that the horses got their fill of it before moving out into the mountains again.

As they started the long climb, following a stream that ran down from the spine of the range, Bennett seemed to make it a point to ride beside the leader. Walters knew there was something the big fellow wanted to say, and he tried to wait until Cleve seemed ready. Finally curiosity got the better of him. He turned slightly in his saddle and asked, "Something bothering you, Cleve?"

Bennett sighed. "Looks as if my wife is going to have to do something about those squaws," he said. "They just don't understand her, and they keep hassling her all the time—stealing from her, pushing her when she passes, just about anything you can think of short of actually attacking her. I think they know better than to try anything quite that bold with her. She told me this morning that she's going to call out Two Big Feet and show them she's not to be trifled with."

Walters almost chuckled. The Ute's wife was well named, and the rest of her matched her feet. But she'd be expecting to fight a woman, not a warrior, and he'd bet she was in for some surprises.

"When does she plan to fight her?" he asked.

"When we camp tonight. Two Big Feet told her this morning that she was going to scalp her and hang her hair on her husband's lance. Just one thing, though. Second

Son wants this to be private—only the woman present. She doesn't intend to shame the woman before the men, but she has to stop this in its tracks."

Bennett looked a bit embarrassed, but Malachi understood at once why the Cheyenne had decided this. It would have been very entertaining, and he regretted missing that battle. Still, he had to agree with her. It didn't pay to have such ruckuses disrupt people who had to go a long way together.

A woman shamed before her man could be extremely bitter and dangerous—Lord knew, Malachi had firsthand experience of that. Creating a feud inside the party would be bad for everyone.

"That's a smart woman you got there," he said. "She understands what's what. We'll pick a good place tonight, where the women can go off safely and get their problems solved once and for all. And I'll make sure nobody wearing pants sneaks off into the rocks to spy on 'em."

Bennett nodded and dropped back into line, as the way narrowed. Cliffs edged out over the stream from both sides, leaving only a lip of stone over which the horses could pass with difficulty. Malachi dismounted to lead his own, and behind him the other members of the party did the same.

After that the country opened out a bit into meadows laced with small bright streams that were lined with willows and aspens. So easy was the going that they came to the high point of the range before nightfall.

Sitting his horse wearily, Walters looked off to the west toward a distant glint that was the surface of the Great Salt Lake that those before him had thought to be a real inland sea. Down there, in a few days' time, they would plan the next stage of this difficult and interesting journey. There had been no major problem, so far, and he hoped the future held nothing very much worse for his band.

Freeman Douglas, his chosen lieutenant, edged up beside him. Malachi pointed down and to the right. "Is that a meadow, Douglas? Think it might be a good place to camp? It looks as if the crick that heads out just below runs right through the middle of it."

Freeman spat a stream of tobacco juice and turned his keen gaze toward the designated spot. "Seems as if. I'll just mosey on down there and check it out before you bring the rest along. Don't want to run into redskins or rattlers, either one, if we kin help it." He nudged his huge gray gelding with one moccasined heel and went on down the track and out of sight along its meandering course.

Malachi turned sideways, resting his butt while he waited. Days in the saddle might make you tough, but you still got mighty tired, he thought. His hind end must be just about turned to leather by now.

A soft tread made him look down to see Cleve Bennett and his wife standing beside the gelding, gazing, in the dying light of the sun, at the faint gleaming line still reflecting from the lake. "That's mighty pretty," Bennett said, his tone awed.

"The Great Bitter Water," Second Son agreed. "I have heard tales about it since I was a small one. Never did I think to see it with my own eyes. It is good that we have come."

She stared up at Malachi. "I hope that this small problem with the wives will not make trouble," she said in a questioning tone.

Walters shook his head, making his long tail of hair

whip in the brisk wind off the height. "You settle that the best way you can, Second Son. We need you. I'll see to it that nobody bothers you while you get things straightened out."

Her smile was somber, and he knew with sudden understanding that she didn't look forward with any pleasure to beating the tarnation out of that hard-nosed Ute woman.

That was the biggest difference he'd seen between her and a regular man. Most men got a kick out of a good fight. According to what he'd been told, she didn't, even though so far she'd invariably won against all comers.

But that was her business. He replied to the whistle from Douglas, signaling that all was well below, and together the three of them headed down in the dying light toward the site of the coming night's confrontation.

chapter
12

It would have been a relatively easy journey from the Green to the Wasatches, Second Son thought, if there had been only the men to contend with. The whites in the Beeville-Walters party were strictly polite to her. Some were even friends who had shared hunting camps or trapping grounds over the years. While she kept her distance from everyone, she felt comfortable with most of those.

The Ute, the Pawnee, and the Yaqui seemed puzzled by her, but they made no problems and ignored her as much as possible. That was good—it was when people didn't ignore her that the Cheyenne warrior seemed to have trouble.

It was the women in the group who became difficult. From the day the two parties joined, back on Bear River, Two Big Feet had shown that she disliked this woman who dared to call herself a man and went hunting with the other men after meat to dry for the future.

There was much hunting to do, for Walters insisted on having plenty of food in hand before they tackled the leaner reaches of their journey. Second Son was one of the more successful hunters, never failing to bring in deer or elk or even moose, and the big Ute woman seemed to resent that furiously. Every time the Cheyenne rode in with game, the woman glared at her as if she had been mortally insulted.

Second Son understood; there were women in her own Burning Heart band who felt the same, and she had always avoided them, when that was possible. She had taken great care not to cross paths with the Ute unless it was unavoidable.

She now felt that had been a mistake. If she had caught the Ute apart from the others and beaten her well, that would have solved the problem for good and all. However, it was too late to think of the past. Now she had to put an end to the constant harassment Two Big Feet had brought upon her from all the other women.

First it had been small things. In the brief pauses for rest, blankets spread to dry on bushes disappeared. At night, moccasins set aside to be mended became so torn or cut that there was no repairing them.

Anytime she turned her back, Second Son found other evidence that Two Big Feet was creating hostility toward her among the wives of trappers and scouts. The others were growing bolder, too, and she had found that the more patient she was with them the worse they became.

She had talked with Cleve about it, wondering what the reactions of the white squaw men would be if she knocked their women about. He assured her that if they had any objections, he would see to the menfolk while she straightened out the women. Still she had hesitated to do anything harsh.

It was only when she found her young mare Shadow suffering with a huge thorn deliberately thrust through the skin of her neck that Second Son called a halt. "I must beat that big Ute woman, Cleve. Will you ask Walters if he objects?"

And now it was time to stop this silliness for good and all. The camp Walters had chosen was a good one, on the flat of a mountain meadow, with plentiful water and patches of wasatch and aspen to provide shelter from the wind rising from the valley.

To the south of the campsite there was a hollow bounded by low ridges that were topped with small trees. It would be a fine place to have her confrontation with Two Big Feet, she thought as the fires were kindled and camps put in order. No one would know what was happening there until it was altogether finished.

Once they had arranged their sleeping blankets and tended their horses, she gestured toward the dark bulk of the ridge nearby. "It is time, I think," she said. "Will you go quietly and tell Walters to keep the men away? I will take that woman into the hollow for her lessoning."

"Don't you want to eat something first?" he asked. The

air was filled with the rich aroma of venison stew from the big pot over the main fire.

She shook her head. "If she has teeth too loose to allow her to eat tonight, it will be a valuable lesson to those she has roused against me. But not even you, Cleve, must watch. I do not want to make a blood enemy, for that is not a wise thing to do."

He nodded agreement. In their risky lives, it was not intelligent to make enemies needlessly. "I'll go and speak to Walters, then," he said. "He can call a meeting or something . . . get all the men together, bent over drawings in the dirt. Nobody will know anything's going on."

She waited and watched as her husband moved to bend over Walters as he sat by the fire. She saw the leader nod and gesture to Freeman.

"Before supper, we'd better choose a route around the lake," Freeman yelled. "Every man come up here and put in your two cents' worth so you won't have any call to bitch if you don't like the way we go."

That made sense, and Second Son almost smiled. She kept still as the men drifted into the circle of firelight to sit in a triple circle, as so many of her own people did.

Only when the last had settled and the rumble of men's voices rose did she stand and go silently to the campsite of Two Big Feet and her Ute husband, Quiet Coyote. She slipped silently to the side of the big woman, who was bent over, securing some leather patches with thongs to her worn deerhide skirt.

"I think we have business, Two Big Feet," Second Son said, keeping her voice quite calm. "Bring the other women, so you will feel more secure. Then I will teach you a valuable lesson that you badly need to learn."

The light of the small fire nearby sparkled in the woman's wide eyes as she jerked upright and stared down at the much shorter Cheyenne beside her. Then her lips curled.

"I will bring the other women to see your humiliation," she said. "Where do you want to go?"

"Over there, out of sight of the men. I would not shame you before your husband," Second Son said yet again. "Come to the hollow with the women. I will be waiting." She turned and melted away silently, as only one with her skills could do, making her way speedily over the ridge and into the small hollow.

The night was not as dark there as she had thought it might be, for there was a sliver of moon sliding down the west. Multitudes of stars brightened the sky for the moment, though in the mountains there was no assurance that a storm would not come up quickly. It was chilly, but she knew that she would soon warm to her work.

She had brought a coal from her own fire in her fire gourd, and with that she lit a torch made of dried grass bound around a branch from one of the small trees. She thrust that into the ground, made another, and touched it to the first.

There must be enough light to fight by. It would also let the other women see for themselves that she was not one to be trifled with when they saw their leader well beaten by one so much smaller than she.

Before long, shadowy shapes began appearing over the ridge, coming into the torchlight. First of all came Two Big Feet, stripped to a loincloth and carrying a club. Her dark skin shone with grease in the reddish glare. So it would not be wise to try grappling with her, even if they were matched in size.

Second Son smiled. The woman thought she was going to allow her to use that club, it was evident. Perhaps even to get her brawny arms around the Cheyenne's much smaller body. But Second Son was too old a warrior for such foolish behavior.

Before Two Big Feet came stamping into the circle of light, Second Son bent for a rock and let fly at the woman's head, knocking her flat. In a moment the club was in Second Son's hand, and she sent it zinging into the darkness.

Then she backed away and gestured for her opponent to rise. Shaking her head, Two Big Feet pushed herself up. She looked a bit dazed, and a thin trickle of blood ran down her face from the spot where the rock had struck her.

Second Son kept a wary eye on her as she began to speak in the odd mixture of tongues that was used among this widely varied group of people. "You do not know the skills of the warrior, Two Big Feet. I will not fight you with weapons. But I will not allow *you* to have weapons, either."

Then she sprang like a puma, tucked together, her entire weight landing solidly at the level of the woman's shoulders. Unbalanced, the Ute went down again with Second Son on top of her.

The Cheyenne did not remain within reach of those brawny arms. Instead she braced one foot, caught a flailing arm as the woman turned over to rise, and heaved the struggling Ute onto her stomach.

Then, sitting on her back, Second Son pounded her head onto the gritty soil of the mountain until she lay still, not even trying to push herself up again. Two Big Feet groaned, and the Cheyenne allowed her to lift her head a bit.

There was a gasp from the watching women as they saw the bruised and bloody face of their leader. As Second Son rose and stepped clear of her victim, the Ute pushed herself up on both hands and then wobbled to her feet, ready, it was plain, to try again.

The smaller woman ducked below her awkward grab at her bound hair and raked the Ute's feet from under her. Two Big Feet went down with a heavy thud. Then Second Son looked up at Standing Bird, wife of the Pawnee scout. "Hand me your knife," she said, and her tone brooked no disobedience.

The woman drew her skinning knife from its sling at her waist and held it hesitantly toward Second Son, her expression terrified. The warrior put her foot on the chest of the gasping Ute and reached for her wild tangle of hair. Not for her the raking with nails and the hair pulling that women usually used, though these people did not understand that. Usually she fought to kill, but this time she had allowed her opponent some leeway. She wanted to teach her, not to kill her.

The women gasped, and Second Son knew they thought she was about to scalp her enemy. That had occurred to her, but she wanted no feud with the Ute scout. There was a better way to teach this hardheaded woman.

She pulled the mass of hair up, bringing its owner with it until she stood on her knees. Then the Cheyenne clumped the strands together and cut the dark tail of hair off as close to the woman's scalp as possible.

This was a ritual scalping, which she had seen once in her youth, among her own people. Its virtue was that the victim did not die but lived to feel the humiliation for a long time to come as the hair grew in straggles over the exposed scalp.

Second Son rose and looked down at the beaten woman. "You are a strong woman, valuable to your man and to our party as a whole. To kill you would be a waste, but to allow you to keep troubling me is not acceptable.

"I leave you your life, with a reminder that you do not wisely gain the wrath of a member of the Burning Heart Cheyenne. Remember, if you would continue to live."

She stepped back and turned to the silent group of women. "You have seen. She is the strongest of you all. If another makes trouble for my camp or my man or for me, and if any other ever harms my mare, I will serve you the same. If we come to the Great Water at last with a party of scalped women, that will be your choice."

Second Son handed the knife back to the Pawnee woman, who took it warily and returned it to the sling. Then the Cheyenne turned back toward the larger meadow, leaving the women to think over what they had seen.

She felt confident that no other among them would choose to face her man and try explaining why her hair was cropped to the scalp. The humor of it struck her as she went, and she muffled a chuckle as she topped the ridge and descended toward her own camping place.

When she returned to her own fire, she glanced toward the big fire and the men, all seemingly intent upon choosing the best route around that bitter water beyond the mountains that barred their way west. Cleve's bright hair gleamed in the firelight as he watched the map drawing and listened to the argument among his peers.

As if feeling her glance upon him, he looked up toward her. She raised a hand to show that her goal had been accomplished, and almost at once he worked his way out of the group by the fire and came to sit beside her.

"You fixed her, eh?" he asked as he dropped onto their bedroll. "And didn't have to kill her? She's an almighty big one. I was afraid—"

"I blooded her face, knocked her breathless, and then I cut off all her hair. She will go with her head down for many moons before it all grows back again." Second Son chuckled again, thinking about that.

Cleve nodded. "Walters'll be glad to see things settle down. The country west of the lake sounds like it's mighty dry and hard to travel. Boon and Knox, over there, tried going that way a while back, just to see what was there, and they say it's dry mountain ranges, patches of desert, no game to speak of, and mighty little water until you come to the big sink where a river runs out of the west and disappears into the desert.

"That's why Walters is waiting in the lower country by the lake, after we get down from here, to let the horses fatten a bit more. He's a great man for taking care of his livestock. Says we can eat them, if it comes down to that." Cleve grimaced at the thought.

That didn't shock Second Son as she knew it did her husband. The Cheyenne were eminently practical when it came to their horses, and if it came to a choice between starvation and eating their mounts, there was no question how they would choose.

She turned as the men began leaving the council fire.

"It is time to sleep," she said. "Tomorrow we must go down a very long way." She gave her deep Cheyenne laugh. "And Two Big Feet will have a cold head all the way."

She covered their small fire with ash and rolled into the blanket beside her man, well pleased with her day's work. There would be no more harassment, she was certain, from the subdued women of the party.

chapter

—13—

The summer was waning, as the party left the grassy slopes flanking the Wasatch Mountains and turned westward. To their left lay the wide water of the salty lake—more of a sea than a lake, Cleve thought. Its briny waters were so thick that he had found it impossible to sink in it while they were camped nearby. Even the nonswimmers in the group had gone into the lake to cool off, and they found they floated like chips.

Walters had insisted upon waiting amid the grass for a week to allow the horses to fatten. That sort of careful attitude reassured Cleve as to the wisdom of joining this expedition. New country was all very well, but death was terribly permanent.

Now the worn mountain ranges lay about them, blistered brown gold in the sunlight, with purple bruises of shadow marking the draws and the shaded areas. The air smelled of dust and something tangy and sharp; Cleve sneezed three times, hard.

Second Son turned to look at him with inquiring eyes, but he shook his head. "Just the dust," he said. "This looks like sorry country to me, warrior. Nothing like the Absarokas, is it?"

For two days they followed the file of horses ahead, listening to the sounds of those behind. Cleve kept gazing off to find the glinting water of the lake from time to time as they came to the tops of the low mountains. It made him feel cooler, somehow, to know that water, even undrinkable water, lay so near and in such quantities.

Once they passed the foot of the range flanking the lake on the west, there was only dry and brittle vegetation, arid grit, salt-tasting dust, and weariness. This was hard country, he decided before they had gone very far.

Now they angled to the south and west, and the country became worse as they went. The cheerful talk and laughter that had accompanied the party thus far died into glum silence, broken only by the irritable snorts of the horses and the clink of metal on metal or the rubbing squeak of leather on leather.

Second Son, used to hard travel, did not droop or complain. Watching her, Cleve had a sudden thought. She was long past her monthly time. Was she pregnant again?

He dropped back a bit, just enough to keep an eye on

her straight back. She rode, as always, with lithe ease, her head turning as her eyes examined everything about their route.

He sighed. He would know when she was ready to tell him. There would be no sign of any kind until then.

Once again he thought of the night their son was born, after Second Son had tricked Jules Terrebonne and fought him to a standstill. She would have killed the thief with her own hands, if Cleve had not roused enough from his own injury to do the job.

As if feeling his gaze, she turned her head, the hard-earned eagle feathers that denoted successful coups fluttering against her cheek. One dark brow quirked questioningly.

Cleve shrugged and heeled Socks into a faster walk until he caught up again. Deep inside, he felt a surge of warmth.

He had enjoyed their son more than he dreamed a man could. Teaching Billy-Wolf to walk, to speak both English and Cheyenne, to ride, to hunt . . . those were things that even Cheyenne fathers did not ordinarily do: their children grew up imitating what they saw their elders do until they were mature enough for the rituals that made them into adults.

Cleve's family had been isolated, the three of them a solid unit, and that had given him the opportunity to watch his son develop. He would like to do that again. Or—he smiled at the thought—to watch a small girl-child turn into the sort of warrior-woman her mother was.

This journey would be very long, very hard for a carrying woman. The physical stress he had seen his wife endure while trapping during the winter when she was expecting her first had taught him a lot about things like that.

No, he couldn't wait for her to get ready. If they were to turn back, it had to be now. They could go to the plains and stay the winter with their son and the Burning Hearts, if that was what she chose. He had to give her the chance.

"Second Son," he said, his voice barely audible above the sound of hooves in dust, "are you pregnant? I have a good reason to ask or I wouldn't say anything right now."

She turned again, surprise in the line of her wide mouth. Then she smiled, and those dark eyes glowed with secret mirth. "And if I should be?" she asked, her tone teasing.

"We could go back, if you want. See your folks. Just if you decide you'd like to, of course," he stammered.

"I will see the Great Water before the child is born," she said. She turned to look toward the sun, now moving down the sky.

"I will see other people and other places. When I return to my people, I will have tales to tell that will rouse great interest among them. Until then, I do not go back."

He grunted. You couldn't put things much plainer than that.

Days passed. From time to time one of the scouts brought word of a spring or a stream still holding a bit of water. Cleve always rode ahead quickly to fill their water skins, for once the thirsty horses arrived, the sharp-tasting water in the scanty holes and streams filled with mud and horse piss.

Walters began riding up and down the line of march, encouraging his party with his own enthusiasm. "Quiet Coyote tells me there's a river down there to the southwest. Runs out of the west, just where we want to go. If we can travel alongside water for a while, I think everybody'll feel a lot better," he told Cleve as they walked together, leading their horses to rest them.

It was a comforting thought. Cleve felt as if his mouth would never taste of anything except alkaline grit and dust tanged with horse manure. Yet he had listened to Smith's tales of that terrible southern route, the salt desert that ate the lives of men and horses. He knew that if they had chosen that way, he would have insisted that Second Son turn back with him.

This was uncomfortable, true, but it was by no means that dangerous to life. There were occasional sources of water, as well as some grass infrequently found in small dells watered by underground springs. The horses were making it fairly well, considering the time of year and the terrain.

So was his wife. She had taken to wearing her robe draped loosely over her shoulders, sheltering in its shade from the devouring sun. When it hid other things, in a month or two, no one would notice anything unusual.

Two Big Feet rode some distance ahead, and Cleve kept a watch on the woman. She had said nothing, done nothing after her defeat at Second Son's hands, but he had no intention of allowing anything she might do to go unnoticed.

Yet she, too, rode silently behind her husband, stoic as were all her people when it came to discomfort or pain. She covered her cropped hair with a leather binding, to his amusement, and she never glanced around to look at her scalper.

Watching her, day after day, Cleve had time to think of

his life among the Cheyenne as well. He had learned something about all the red-skinned people. They lived in places and ways that few whites would consent to endure. Comfort and pleasure were so seldom known that they did not miss those things, only enjoying them to the fullest when they found them.

He came to admire the big Ute and her small, wiry man as they moved steadily toward a goal that held nothing in particular for them. The scout was a silent person, going and coming without comment, when there was need. Now that his wife had stopped deviling Second Son, she, too, was silent and unwavering.

Quiet Coyote's reports to Walters, issued in his broken bits of English, were marvels of brevity. As the party moved through the harsh world in which they found themselves, Cleve found also that those reports were entirely accurate.

The sun slid a bit toward the south as summer waned, and the long reaches of ridges, alkali flats, and dry scrub stretched before the travelers as if they would never end. From time to time there was a water hole, tainted at this time of year with bitterness. The horses nibbled sage and brush, for there was no grass except tan stubble in sheltered spots.

It seemed to Cleve that the long file of riders, the string of packhorses, the laden mounts of the Indian guides and squaws would travel forever over this impossible land, though the appearance of a river comforted the journey a bit.

As he was beginning to wonder if he would live long enough to see the Pacific Ocean, a dim jumble of shapes came into view at the edge of the horizon. Not hills, not exactly trees, the blurred images trembled into and out of focus.

Dust filled Cleve's nostrils and made him blink to clear his irritated eyes. Now he realized that real trees loomed amid the blurs. After a long while he saw that those ahead were riding down into a great sink. As he went in his turn there were occasional streams, even pools of water beginning to come into focus in the distance.

On they rode, and the land became swampy, with large areas grown with tules among which he suspected might live frogs and snakes and perhaps other edible creatures. Even as he thought that, the Ute straightened on his roan and turned his head; he and his woman stared to the left, and at that moment Second Son dropped back and spoke over her shoulder.

"There are people around us. I smell them."

How she could smell anything with a nose full of swampy stinks was something Cleve couldn't understand. Yet he knew what must be done, and he kicked Socks into a trot and moved up the long line of riders to the distant head of the line.

Walters rode just behind the Pawnee scout, with Beeville some lengths behind him. He looked back as Cleve came up. "What is it?" the small man asked. From his tone, Cleve knew that he had seen something strange himself.

"Second Son smells people. I don't see them. She doesn't see them, or she'd have said so. But if she smells them, they're there. What do we do?"

Walters let out a long breath and raised his hand to halt the long column. Beeville kneed his own horse up to join his lieutenant and Bennett.

The Pawnee turned his mount between his strong knees

and rode back to make part of the group. "Men here," he said. Now he stretched a long arm ending in a pointing finger. "See—there."

Walters raised his spyglass and adjusted it to scan slowly across the deceptive country they must cross. Even as he nodded, discovering what he was searching for, Cleve found himself looking into a pair of eyes, much closer, that he had thought might be dark pebbles lying amid the rushes.

"Diggers?" Beeville asked.

"Paiute," agreed the Pawnee.

Fascinated, Cleve watched the shape he had spotted as it curled against the earth, still hidden by the reeds, it thought, from those it was observing. Squinting, he let his gaze drift over the gray-green-tan countryside, ignoring details, just letting colors and shapes enter his mind.

Another man-shape popped into view, and another. He nudged his horse closer to Walters's and touched the leader's arm. "We're going right through an entire tribe of 'em," he said.

"Yes," said the Pawnee. "All around now. All behind, too. They will follow."

In the silence that followed his deep voice, Cleve heard a whistle from Second Son. Twice, once, three times in quick succession.

"That means keep a close watch—there might be danger," he said in a conversational tone.

Cleve turned to check on his wife, and to his astonishment he saw that a ragged line of walkers had fallen in behind the riders, just within the range of visibility. "We have visitors back there," he said. "What do they want?"

The Pawnee looked down his hooked nose and said

nothing. He hated to admit that there might be something he didn't know. Walters signaled to Quiet Coyote, and the Ute heeled his horse into a trot to join them at the head of the now stationary column.

Again, Walters asked Cleve's question. The Ute laughed, that harsh note that seemed devoid of humor until you knew something about Indians. "They see many things," the scout said. "Those men got no horse, no gun. Got no lodge, no pot, no blanket. Got nothing."

"Well?" Walters looked puzzled.

The Ute sighed with frustration as he seemed to search his small store of English for more words. He turned to Cleve and spouted a stream of very passable Cheyenne.

Bennett listened intently. At once he understood the situation and the possibility of trouble, if things were not handled with some finesse.

He turned to Walters and Beeville. "He says that these people have never in their lives seen so many possessions. They have nothing, and most of the things we have they don't understand and couldn't use if they had them. But they're interested—I guess you could say they're fascinated.

"The Ute says they'll follow until we stop. There are a lot more of them than we might think, too. Then they'll lie down all around our camp and watch what we do. He says they'll come along every step of the way like starving dogs until something happens to make them stop. He says to watch them, if we want to keep what we have."

Beeville, who seldom said much, coughed meaningfully. Walters, as if understanding just what he meant, shrugged.

"Then we'll go ahead as if they're not there at all, and when the time comes, we'll decide what to do about 'em.

By God, here we get almost to the river, and this comes up. Can't win for losin', I guess." He signaled for the riders to proceed, and Cleve fell in behind him, thinking hard.

Nobody could live for long in the country they'd just crossed. It had to be this unexpected wetland that allowed these naked, earth-colored people to survive at all. He watched them from the corner of his eye as more rose from their hiding places.

You could count their ribs. Hell, if you ran a stick along them, they'd rattle like running a walking stick down the splits of a rail fence.

People that lean and hungry might be dangerous, given the chance, though they seemed to carry nothing more threatening than digging sticks and awkward stone knives. Still, Cleve determined that he'd watch them closely. He didn't intend for his wife and the baby she carried to risk anything he might prevent.

chapter

—14—

Ate Two Rabbits had been curled in the shade of a rock ledge and a cottonwood, telling stories to himself about fat snakes and lizards ready for the catching or large rabbits falling into his quick hands. There was a lot of time for tale telling, because he had nothing at all to do when he wasn't hungry.

With no place to store food, there would have been no point in working hard to build up supplies of it. Besides, food was so scanty that anyone who tried such an unusual thing would starve someone else. Such large thoughts sometimes troubled the mind of Ate Two Rabbits, making his head hurt.

He pushed away those ideas and told himself the old tale of Sky Woman, who traveled from one horizon to the other, round and golden at times, skinny and bent at others, as if she lived a new life from youth to age on a regular basis. From so high, she could see everything that happened in the world, and he often invented other tales about the things she might have learned while making her long journey.

He thought of his last woman, Digs with Fingers, dead now with the child she had been bearing. She, too, had been round—or at least rounder than the average woman of his kind.

She had never had the opportunity to grow old, although Ate Two Rabbits was nearing three double hands of summers and already felt the twinges of age in his bones. His teeth had loosened in the past winter, and he knew that all too soon he would wither to sticklike bones and leather skin. Then he would die, as his people's old ones did, when winter brought starvation and coughing sickness into their scanty lodges.

Of the three babies Digs with Fingers had brought into the world, only one survived. Broken Hand, her daughter, was growing old herself, her teeth scanty, her breasts sagging. She had lived longer now than her mother, and she had borne six sons, two of whom still lived.

Sometimes it occurred to that strange old man who lived in the head of Ate Two Rabbits to wonder why he and his kind struggled so hard to stay alive. There was little comfort in his life now that Digs with Fingers was gone. Children grew large enough to fend for themselves and scattered across the land to scavenge what they could. There was not even an old man nearby to share tales and questions.

It had been many suns since Ate Two Rabbits had spoken with a human being, although he kept up a running conversation with the lizards living in the same shelter with him. He was telling the big spotted fellow, who might become his next meal, the Sky Woman story yet again when something strange and alien caught his ear.

The man paused, listening. Then he crept out of the shade and stood, head cocked to hear better. Things jingled in tones he had never heard before. The sound of horses' hooves was one he knew, for other tribes came that way at times, but the accompanying sounds were strange and disturbing.

He pulled his combination digging stick and lance out of the burrow and climbed onto the top of his rock to see better. Then he almost doubted his own keen senses.

A long line of riders was crossing the dry lands. Things attached to their horses shone brighter than mica in rock, and they carried other tools or weapons in their hands or on their backs. Not lances. Not digging sticks.

Enthralled, the aging man leaped down from his perch and ran toward that line, now hidden by the growth between. When he topped the last ridge, he lay flat and stared as those riders passed in the distance.

Behind them he could see distant figures who were of his own kind, drawn as he had been to this wonder. Ate Two Rabbits dropped to hands and knees and scampered like a lizard across the rough, prickly ground toward the end of the file.

Along the way he met no fewer than six others who

were on the same mission. They did not pause to speak but hurried on, hidden in the swamp's bushes and reeds, until they were near enough to see the passing marvels clearly.

He lay flat, invisible, he felt, to anyone but one of his own people. The others settled nearby; all gazed wide-eyed at the laden horses, the riders clad in undreamed-of riches of cloth and fur and leather.

When the column halted, Ate Two Rabbits wondered at first what had caused that to happen. Then he realized that other red-skinned people rode with the group. It must be their keener senses that had detected the presence of the Real People.

There was one among those alien people whose hair hung in a long braid beneath his leather hat. When his head turned, those locks shone with a brilliance that rivaled the sun. What sort of man could this be? A god?

But Ate Two Rabbits had lived too long to believe in gods of any kind. No, this was a man of some breed, and those beside him, strange though they might seem, were men as well. There were women, also, among those riding at the rear of the column.

That excited him. The women of the Real People lived short lives, and there were always men without wives among his kind. Was there a way to steal these women? Those men had great wealth and could buy more when they returned to the place they had come from.

The magical beings sat their horses for some time, and when they began looking about them, Ate Two Rabbits knew they had seen the Real People coming from far and near to see this wonder. He rose to his feet, brushed the grit from his knees and elbows, and moved toward the others who were following the column.

Broken Hand was among them, carrying her surviving child slung on her back with straps of snakeskin. She looked much like her mother, with big eyes under arched brows. Her lips were sunken where her teeth had been knocked out with stones as they decayed, but still her face reminded him of better days.

He fell in beside her and teased the small boy on her back by tickling him with strands of dried grass. Children were always amusing, though one had to understand that they would probably die before they grew very big.

Ahead, the column moved forward, the increasing stands of willows hiding the riches and the riders. Already Ate Two Rabbits was thinking of ways to get his hands on anything he could find. When he spotted Owl Claw among another approaching group of the Real People, he left off tickling his grandson and moved to intercept the old man.

Of all the Real People, Owl Claw had lived longest and learned the most. His summers counted at least five double hands, and his skin had a collection of scars and wrinkles worthy of one who had attained such a great age. His wits were still sharp, although his eyes had lost some of their keenness, and it took a moment before he recognized Ate Two Rabbits.

The younger man grunted a greeting. "Have you seen their possessions?" he asked, his tone guarded. "Can you see the bright things they carry on their horses and in their hands?"

Owl nodded. "Even these eyes can see those sparks like lightning in the night sky. I have smelled alien people and heard a language that I have never known before. Those who are not pale skins are kinds I have known in the past. A Ute, a Pawnee, a Yaqui from the south I recognize.

"There is another that I do not know. It rides like a man, watches like a man, but my nose tells me that it is a woman, even at such a distance."

Ate Two Rabbits peered through the bushes, but his eyes could not find that bright-haired rider he had noticed. "I would like to have some of those treasures," he said, looking obliquely at Owl. "Is there a way to approach those people, do you think?"

The older man shook his head. "Not too quickly. We will watch when they camp. We will keep our eyes upon them. If there is a chance to creep in and take things, then we will be ready. But we must seem quiet and friendly.

"We must not make them wary. Though I do not know this with certainty, I suspect that those long sticks in their hands are weapons of some kind."

Ate Two Rabbits fondled his stone-headed ax. He had killed small animals with it often, and he had even used it against others of the Real People, when the situation warranted. Skulls crushed easily beneath its solid weight.

"If we could throw rocks at them, we might bring down enough of the men to allow us to carry away the women," he mused, as if to himself.

"True." Owl seemed to be considering that possibility. "Our people are very accurate throwers of rocks. Our axes and lances are effective against the things we know. But these are people we do not know. We must be cautious, Ate Two Rabbits. We must be subtle."

• • •

The sun moved down behind the western ranges. Now the column neared the river, with its richness of willows and cottonwoods, its nearby flocks of birds. Small game drank there, and always one could find prey in times of scarcity. But not one of the Real People overhunted the place. It was their emergency source of food in time of need.

When the riders camped, Ate Two Rabbits was hidden among the willows, watching everything the strangers did. Beside him was the nephew of Owl and the older son of Broken Hand. All lay flat, determined not to betray their presence as these others settled for the night.

Voices rose as a great fire was lighted, using dead branches from fallen trees that grew in this watered country. Soon a savory smell filled the air, and the watching People found their mouths watering. Never had Ate Two Rabbits dreamed of any food that smelled so good.

The stranger women in the new camp made ready for the night, unrolling thick mats of skin. The Digger had never seen a blanket of any kind. Rabbit or antelope skins sewn together to make a scanty covering for his bones in winter were the best he had ever known. The thought of the warmth and comfort those strangers had filled his heart with envy.

Guards were posted on each side of the camp, the river forming a barrier behind it and an arm of the swampy ground making approach from the north very difficult. The newcomers kept gazing about warily, watching those of the Real People who had not slipped away or hidden.

The ground was overgrown with grasses and weeds, nourished by the wet soil. That offered ample cover, and

Ate Two Rabbits picked out his route as he waited for the last fire to be damped.

At last all was silent except for the stamp and snort of an occasional horse. One fire burned in the middle of the camp, but its circle of light did not reach far enough to hinder a clever thief. As cleanly as any lizard, the Digger slid into the growth and moved noiselessly toward the edge of the circled sleepers.

He knew that the two boys were also moving, but there was no sound to betray that fact. They could aim for their own goals—his was the place where that golden-haired man had lain beside the strange person who seemed a man but was in fact a woman. Such magical people must have powers that were even more wonderful than the possessions of the others in their group.

Although nothing gave warning that it was true, he knew that others of his kind were also creeping into that camp, their fingers itching for the riches to be found there. Who knew? Perhaps he might return from this night's raid with another wife. If he was very skillful and very lucky, he might carry away that man-woman to be his own.

He froze against the earth as one of the scouts passed near, moccasins silent against the soil. Even the Yaqui, he thought, grinning, could not detect his presence.

He passed other sleeping people, men and some women, but he did not encumber himself with treasures that might clink and jingle as he carried them. When he returned he might be burdened with that woman as well. No, one treasure, a new wife, was enough for one night.

At last he neared the spot he had marked in his mind. An ancient cottonwood leaned above the place his quarry had chosen to rest, and it made a perfect marker against the starry sky. When he drew very near, he froze again, listening to the breathing of those who slept there.

A harsh exhalation told him that the man was to his right. Lighter breathing, steady and quiet, marked the location of the woman on the left.

Ate Two Rabbits felt about him, his fingers careful as they ran over the neatly piled equipment near the feet of the sleepers. There were more blankets made of fur and hides. Metal things were also there, long shapes and rounded ones, and he had no idea what they might be.

But it was a blanket that he needed to silence and control the woman. He drew the thick folds free of the stack and moved toward the pale glimmer that was her face in the starlight. He paused for a moment, staring at the smooth oval, incredibly unmarred. She must be very young, he thought, to lack scars and wrinkles.

Moving with catlike swiftness, he placed the thickness over her length, face and all, and rolled her in its folds. The man next to her did not stir, so silent had been the attack.

The woman had surely waked, but to the surprise of her kidnapper she did not struggle, did not move, did not try to cry out. Congratulating himself upon finding so docile a spouse, the Digger began the long retreat through the sleeping party. Again he froze as the Ute passed, on watch, alert, yet unable to see the thief so near his passing feet.

Bit by bit, the man withdrew from the camp, never tempted to try for some other trophy. This was what he wanted, and he was more than content.

When he came outside the perimeter again, he pulled the limp bundle into the shelter of a clump of bushes. Panting, he lay flat beside it, filled with triumph. Tomorrow he would gloat over those who stole only shining trinkets.

Something made him turn his head. Light glinted off a bright blade slicing through the blanket's folds. The woman emerged instantly, and before he could move, Ate Two Rabbits was in her grasp, struggling for his life.

The last thing he felt was that beautiful metal blade as it bit through his throat and severed his jugular. Then all his hungers ended forever.

chapter

—15—

The smell of green things tanged the air, a welcome scent to the riders as they descended into the sink that contained the river. They stopped in the shelter of cottonwood and willow growth, and Second Son slid from Shadow, moving at once along the line of their pack animals, loosing the bindings to ease the supplies off their sweaty backs.

About her there was the normal bustle as the travelers went about making camp. Designated cooks and fire builders gathered wood and kindled the main cookfire, but she and Cleve preferred to eat together in their own chosen sleeping place.

While Cleve led the horses down to the water, she built their own small fire and spitted above it the rabbits that had fallen to her arrows earlier in the day. Crouching there, she felt the pressure of eyes watching her and all the others about her.

The all but invisible circle of watchers beyond the perimeter of the camp made her cautious. Second Son knew nothing of these starved and dusty people, but the look of them was disquieting, and their silent ranks, following the column, somehow filled her with a sense of impending danger.

Beeville, according to Cleve, discounted the Diggers as a weak people, armed only with stone-headed axes and wooden lances. "He says there's no way they could be any hazard to as big and well armed a group as this one," he had said when he returned from consulting with the leaders of the party.

But as she turned each rabbit on its stick, she was thinking about the multitudes of hidden, glittering eyes that even now watched every move made in the encampment. Her skin prickled with unease, even when Cleve returned after turning the hobbled horses into the riata-and-stake-enclosed pen over against the riverbank.

"Those people—they want what we have," she said to her husband as they sat cross-legged and began eating dripping bits of rabbit. "I feel it in my heart. There will be intruders into the camp tonight."

"Don't worry." He grinned at her over the tiny fire, his face greasy and gleaming. "Beeville and Walters have set the Indian scouts to guard the camp, along with several of the best shots. Those fellows don't miss seeing anything, and the riflemen don't miss hitting anything. You can sleep without keeping one eye open, I think, with them on patrol."

Although she should have been reassured, Second Son had led too many raids of her own to believe that any guard could keep a determined warrior away. Yet with Cleve beside her, solid and warm in his blanket roll, she fell asleep at last, even the minor nausea that seemed to accompany her pregnancies failing to keep her awake.

She woke suddenly and completely when a thick mass plopped over her, covering her from face to feet. Someone was rolling her into a helpless bundle so quickly that there was no time to do anything. Immediately her attacker began pulling her over the ground, so silently that even she could hear nothing except the faint rasp of the gritty grass beneath the heavy hide blanket that confined her.

So. She was being stolen, herself. An interesting idea, and one that promised a rude shock for the person daring to do this. She slid her right hand, which had been beside her hip, over and down to the place where her thong sling held her fine metal knife. She slept with it at her side always, even in the most secure circumstances.

As her kidnapper tugged her across the ground, still silently and with frequent pauses to avoid detection, she worked the knife into position and began slicing cautiously through the first layer of the rolled blanket that confined her.

Time passed with dreamlike slowness as the man pulled her along, seemingly limp as a corpse, to his unknown goal. Always her knife was busy, its motions barely perceptible. The first layer was open the length of her forearm; the second was yielding to the persistent blade.

When the motion stopped at last, she knew that she was almost ready to emerge like a butterfly from its cocoon, knife in hand rather than damp wings making ready to unfold.

She listened, still busy with the knife, to the harsh breathing of the one beside her. He was distracted by his own weariness, she knew.

At once she sliced herself free and was upon him, her legs still entangled in the blankets but her powerful arms able to handle the man's ropy muscles and hard hands as they struggled. She turned him at last, moving him to meet her blade.

Second Son stood in the shelter of the bush, looking carefully at the starlit river, the overgrown basin into which it flowed, the shadowy shapes of the trees beneath which her companions slept. "Aiiiiyeee!" she shrilled. "Wake and look to yourselves!"

The men in the party were old hands, and their red women and the scouts were impossible to surprise into a lack of caution. There were no shouts, no screams; instantly a feeling of tension filled the place. Then small yelps told of intruding Diggers who found themselves caught at their pilfering.

She strode back toward camp, to the spot where someone had already put new fuel onto the coals of the big fire. Dark shapes were also moving in that direction from all points, some dragging struggling Diggers. As she came into the light of the newly rekindled blaze, she realized that quick feet were fleeing all around her.

"They are all about us!" she said to Walters, who was standing, his flintlock in hand, staring at the confused mix of shadow and firelight that was his formerly peaceful camp.

Even as she spoke a horse screamed; several broke free of the makeshift pen and bucked their way out of the camp, trying, Second Son could see, to shake free of the wiry bodies clinging to their manes and backs and tails.

Again she cried out into the darkness, "The horses! They are taking the horses!"

She ran, leaping over groggy bodies of men trying to wake, over piles of goods and supplies, plowing through knots of people subduing the thieves they had caught. Then Cleve was beside her, his hand touching her shoulder to tell her he was there.

"Socks?" he panted. "You see if they got him?"

"No." She paused beside the broken strands of the rope fence. "There is Shadow. I see two—three of the packhorses. No Socks."

At once, Cleve turned and whistled the old signal that had been taught to this successor of his faithful old mount. Again he whistled, more shrilly, and from a distance Second Son heard the answering whinny of the stallion, followed by a scream of terror.

As one, the pair moved toward the sound. Hooves pounded toward them as Socks leaped a small runnel leading toward the river and bowled aside anyone in his path as he came to join his master.

On his back, terrified, crouched an Indian, his hands wound so tightly into the animal's mane that he could not get them loose. Second Son used her still-bloody knife to cut the coarse hair free, as Cleve jerked the skinny man off the stallion's back.

The big fire was now roaring with fresh fuel, and by its light the Cheyenne could see a long gash scarring the horse's side. "They would have eaten him, I think," she said. "They do not know about horses, but they do understand an animal big enough to provide a lot of meat."

Cleve growled, but he seemed strangely gentle as he set the emaciated form of the Digger on its feet and looked into the dusty-gray face. "I don't blame 'em," he said. "Look at this poor bastard! He hasn't enough meat on him to say grace over. My God, how do these people live out here?"

Looking at the man from the alien viewpoint she had learned to impose upon herself, Second Son could see what Cleve meant. These were pitiful creatures, their bones almost poking through their skins. Only in the very worst of the winters of famine had she ever seen her own people so emaciated.

Someone among the travelers yelled, "Let's hang these horse thieves!"

Walters appeared among the disturbed group, walking quietly as always, his face calm. "No," he said. "We are in their country. They know nothing about us, but they see that we're fat and we've got a lot of things they never dreamed about. You can't blame 'em any more than a bunch of children if they want to come in and grab what they see.

"It's never a good idea to make enemies in new country that you might need to travel over coming back. These folks know this country, and an ambush can kill us just as dead with rock slides as it can with lead bullets." He looked around, catching the eyes of the men who had come with ropes.

"Never cut off your line of retreat, boys. It's just not good business. Now run these poor varmints out of camp and let's try to get some sleep. If we kill 'em, you never know what sort of nasty surprise the rest might spring on us as we travel."

Second Son nodded. He made sense, that one. Indeed, she had learned much from watching him handle his men and the horses as the group moved over the mountains and the desert. Now she realized that there were other ways than attack that could be used in dealing with strange tribes. It was something she would remember.

The men who had gone after the horses returned with the snorting, frightened animals. Only some half dozen had escaped before those nearest the pen rose to calm the herd, but those returned to camp were terrified; all showed knife scars.

The Diggers must have been trying to carve meat from the living beasts. That was something that shocked even the practical Cheyenne, who had eaten her share of horse meat when following a hard trail through hungry country.

By the time the camp calmed at last, it was very late. A raddled remnant of moon had risen in the east, its reddish rays making the water gleam like blood and the surrounding countryside take on a ghostlike air. Second Son shivered as she rolled into her new blanket and backed against Cleve's bulk.

For an instant she thought she felt a tiny flutter in her body, as if, even so young, the child she carried was disturbed. But it was too soon. It would be a long time yet before her baby kicked at her side.

She closed her eyes, knowing that this time a line of fires edged the camp, even on the side next to the river. Their glow shone pink through her eyelids, but behind her eyes she saw again the skinny shape of the Paiute, the ribs like sticks pushing through the dusty skin.

No, even in times of hunger, when the winter ran long and supplies became scanty, her own Burning Heart Cheyenne had never looked like that. She wondered about the women among the Diggers. How did they keep their infants alive and their children fed until they were old enough to scavenge for themselves? Lizards and snakes were not proper food for the very young.

She shivered against Cleve, thinking of her son in such circumstances. And the baby, still only a seed in her belly. What would she do if she must live as these people did, with only the roots and seeds and snakes and lizards caught each day standing between her and death? Her unborn child and its death?

It was a sobering thought, and she felt a sudden regret for the man she had killed so quickly out there beyond the fires. He had taken her, not the weapons or pots or blankets. Had he lost a wife that he tried to replace?

What a pity for him that he had chosen a warrior, rather than a woman who would shrug and survive, no matter who her man was or where they lived together. That sort of patience had never been hers, and she wondered how her sisters-in-law and the women of her fellow travelers managed it.

But then—she sighed and turned, feeling darkness begin to fill her mind—she had never been a woman in any way that mattered. Except to Cleve. She smiled as she drifted into sleep.

chapter

— 16 —

Malachi Walters realized that he had misjudged the Diggers who followed his train. After that first night of confusion and infiltration, he made certain that fresh shifts of watchers went on duty every four hours, and he secured the horses even more carefully. Those acquisitive people had hurt a couple of the beasts so badly after they broke free that they had to be destroyed.

Freeman Douglas wanted to burn the carcasses, but Malachi had seen those picket-fence ribs, the gaunt faces with eyes glittering with hunger. He couldn't bear to waste that amount of meat, and there was no time at this point to stop and dry it. They had to cross those mountains Smith had told him about before the snows grew deep on the passes.

"Leave it for 'em," he said, although he knew all too well this might make for future problems with the Paiute. "They've got little ones with 'em. We need to move, anyway. But watch our flanks—we don't want to lose any more horses. Put good men to herd the spare mounts."

He turned to find Cleve Bennett leading up his loaded horses. "We'll be ready in half a shake," the trapper said. "Second Son's got the saddle horses in hand. She was a bit sleepy this morning. Had an exciting night." He grinned, but Walters saw the remnant of worry in his pale eyes.

"We all did, but it'd have been a sight more excitin' if she hadn't yelled when she did. We'd have lost a bunch of livestock. Guns, knives—no tellin' what those skinny bastards would have left with, if we hadn't waked up."

He shook his head. "The scouts're really angry. Quiet Coyote offered to give up right here and take his wife home, if I wanted. Felt he'd let us down."

Bennett shrugged. "If I could sleep right through having my wife kidnapped from under my arm, I can't blame the Ute for missing those sneaky critters.

"Once you think about it, they've got to creep up on lizards and snakes and mice. Got to be almighty quiet and quick, which was proved to my satisfaction last night. We intend to take turns watching until we get beyond their range."

That sounded like a good idea, even with shifts of watchmen securing the boundaries. "I think we'll ask the rest to do the same. We can't resupply if we lose something really important," Walters said.

"We got to keep what we have and move fast now. Smith and his bunch got snowed in up in the Sierras on their way back and almost didn't make it out again. It's getting late in the year now, and we need to get over the snow line and down into the lowlands before winter sets in."

Many of the band had also heard tales of those dagger-toothed mountains to the west, and there was no protest when they moved out immediately, leaving the two dead horses for the Diggers. Walters felt the meat might delay those who had been following, and he badly wanted to be rid of them.

People seemed to be people wherever they lived and however no-account they looked, he was learning. They had abilities that came through for them, even the most primitive, and he should have recalled that from his travels among the mountain tribes farther east. He never mentioned it to other white men, but he'd found that men who didn't wear two-legged pants tended to be able to think just about as well as those who did.

They rode out of camp, following the river that drained into this basin from the southwest. Having a water supply close at hand would make their journey far easier, he knew, although it might also mean that they would encounter more native people along the way.

In the desert country, water drew living things to it. The possibility of finding other Indians was outweighed by the likelihood of also finding game.

They went west and south, along its course. They camped the first night in a flat spot edged by broken cliffs to north and east and the river on the south. It was easy to watch and to defend, but no one came. Evidently the Diggers were feasting on the dead horses.

The next morning, before noon, one of the herdsmen at the tail of the horse herd came riding up fast beside Walters and Beeville. "They're back there," he said, and sneezed. Once they left the swampy sink, the dust of that rear position made it one that nobody could take for long at a stretch.

"How many?" asked Beeville, craning to look back along the line of riders.

"Can't tell, so far. But I can see a bunch of little bitty shapes back there, and they're runnin' to catch up. By damn, they're doin' it, too. They'll be around our camp again by dark, Mr. Beeville, if I'm not crazy."

Walters sighed. He'd wondered . . . but this didn't surprise him. He had seen warriors run for unbelievable distances and fight like demons at the end of their journeys.

The herdsman dropped back along the line, and Walters signaled to Douglas. "Ride ahead and get the scouts to pick another defensible campsite," he said. "Looks as if we're goin' to have company again."

They moved steadily, walking and riding, walking and riding, then pausing to water the horses and to eat before riding some more. The terrain was rough, but they covered a lot of distance before the sun touched the high ridges ahead.

The Yaqui met the leaders of the train beside a narrow trail that cut off a bend in the river. "Camp there," he said, gesturing up the steep-walled ravine.

Walters dropped to one side, letting Beeville lead the way into the defile. He remained beside the Yaqui, watching as the long string of men and mounts and Indian women approached and disappeared into the cut.

When Bennett and his wife drew level, he called, "They're goin' to be here for supper. Better watch out, Miz Bennett!"

Although she had not understood the teasing of white men at the beginning, she had begun to respond in kind, after traveling with the group for so long. She smiled back, a narrow quirk of the lips.

"Perhaps I will capture a wife for myself again," she replied. "Two sharing the work would be better, maybe."

Walters almost choked. He'd heard the tale, from Cleve himself, about how she'd ridden out of her Burning Heart village after her man, determined to get him as her "wife." She was coming along, that woman. Not many *white* women would have appreciated the humor of her courtship with Bennett.

When the last spare horse had been driven into the narrow space by the dusty men at the end of the train, Walters kicked his horse into motion and followed the Yaqui along the echoing slot between faces of rock.

Already the dust smelled of urine and dung. It was good to come into the air again and find a campsite that was ideal for his purposes.

The river swung back beyond the bastion of stone, and its waters washed the other end of this opening. The wide part lay between the very narrow outlet and a much wider inlet, a rock-strewn path that seemed to follow the verge of the river on the western end.

Already the first-comers had kindled the big cookfire. In this confined space, smaller fires would be impractical, but those men with squaws were already discussing a schedule for the watch, while those without made their own sleeping places ready for the night and tended their own horses.

Bennett and Second Son were squatting with Freeman Douglas, who had been drawing in the dust. "If you put some men up there," said Cleve, pointing up toward a prow of rock that loomed over the camp, "They'll keep anybody from dropping into the middle of us."

Second Son, who seldom spoke but always had something important to say when she did, said, "If I were those men behind, I would creep up the rough way to that edge above us. Then I would watch very close.

"When there was a chance, and there always is a chance, I would climb down one of those crannies and steal what I wanted. Then I would run and jump into the river."

She glanced about at the other men. "I have made many raids, stolen many horses. This is how I would do it."

"Good enough for me," said Walters, coming out of the darkness into the firelight. "Let's put men here, here, and here," he said, dotting marks into Douglas's diagram. "Then might as well put a few more up there to watch us from above. We've already seen how those Diggers can slip through alert watchmen. We'd better stop up all the holes we can find."

Walters didn't sleep well. He kept feeling someone watching him, and he knew he would not have felt the gazes of his own men. Someone, prevented from approaching the edge and descending by the three Indian scouts who had been placed there, was keeping a close eye on the camp from much higher on the rocky heights.

He was glad when the sky lightened, and he could get up and put the huge coffeepot near the uncovered coals of last night's fire. Before he got back from the river with a bucket of water, Douglas and Beeville had risen, yawning and bleary-eyed, to squat beside the new blaze, warming their hands from the chill of the desert night.

"Well, we made it without anybody getting through," Beeville grunted, holding the pot steady while Walters poured the water in. He pushed it near the fire, and the spatters of damp began to hiss and sputter.

Coffee and jerky were the usual breakfast fare, and that took very little time to prepare and consume. Before the sun topped the cliffs, the file was riding onward, following the sliver of trail along the water, while dislodged shards of stone splashed into the river.

There was no way to tell if anyone shadowed their route on the high ground above, but Walters was thankful to have gained another day on these persistent pursuers. Like mosquitoes, they seemed impossible to discourage.

There was no sound to indicate anyone near, either on the heights or following behind the bends of the river, though the scouts took turns checking. Before noon, Walters paused to water the horses and signaled for Quiet Coyote to approach.

"No sign?" he asked the Ute.

Coyote grunted. "They there," he said. "Just not see."

As that was Malachi's own opinion, he felt sure it was the truth. "I'd like to get out of this before we camp for the night," he said. "We need to cover ground fast now, if we're not to get caught in the high country. Besides, in this mess of rocks and ravines, they could be all over us before we knew it."

Coyote gave a jerk of his chin. "I go fast," he said. "Find way out. Find camp place. All right?"

It was just what Malachi had hoped for, though he hated to spare one of the scouts, with the Diggers still an unknown quantity on their heels. "You go on ahead, Quiet Coyote. I'll bring on the bunch as fast as we can make it. See if you can find a good spot to defend, if you can."

He knew that last request was unnecessary. The Indians in his group seemed more disgusted by the Paiute than their white companions. If a defensible place existed, Coyote would find it.

They kept riding, walking, riding, and at last Walters saw a break ahead, where the river canyon widened into a great V-shape. Beyond, there seemed to be only sky, and he hurried his band toward that more open country.

He emerged to see a distant rider moving toward him over broken scrubland. "Coyote," he said.

Cleve Bennett, riding beside him at this point, shaded his eyes, then nodded. "He looks pretty satisfied. If he'd found trouble, he'd be hightailing it for home right about now."

The Ute met them beyond the mouth of the canyon and pointed off to the north. "Big flat space there. No tree, no bush. Only mound, very small, of little animal. Can see anything that move, all right? Good place to camp. No cover for Paiute."

He was right. You couldn't have hidden a prairie dog on the top of the ground, though the numerous mounds showed that the little creatures must live beneath it in considerable numbers. They'd add meat for the pot without sending out hunters, Walters realized. Not a bad arrangement, if you liked prairie-dog stew.

It turned out that most of the company agreed it was delicious, after the Indians, including Second Son, laid siege to the prairie-dog village and skewered a bunch of the quick little animals with silent arrows. The big pot over the fire simmered, sending out wonderful smells as the cook threw in handfuls of sage, gathered as they traveled.

Before the last light left the sky, however, the camp was ringed, once again, with silent, watching Diggers. There was something different about them this time, something ominous.

Walters had a sudden, disturbing thought. "Nobody back at the rear had any tangle with the Diggers, did they? Today or before now?"

Toosh Marlow, sitting on a rock with his boot in his hand, looked up and his face reddened. "I reckon I did," he said. "Yesterday. A horse got loose from the bunch, and I rid back a ways to bring him in. One of them rascals jumped him with a knife in his hand, and I shot him before he could ruin the animal. I think I kilt him. He didn't even twitch, once he fell."

Walters leaned back against his saddle and thought hard. Was this a party looking for vengeance? Second Son had, she told him, killed the man who stole her out of camp, but that should be long enough ago now to rule out retaliation. This was another matter.

"I don't blame you for shootin' the varmint," he said to Toosh, "but I sure wish you hadn't had to. And I wish you'd have told me. I think we've got us a bunch of riled Injuns all around us."

Second Son, who had made her camp close to the main cookfire, looked up and her gaze met his. "I think you are correct," she said in her curiously precise English that

Cleve had taught her. "I think they intend to attack, but not in the way we expect. Take care, Mr. Walters. They are devious people, I think."

He wished he didn't agree with her so completely. As it was, he set enough guards to keep half the camp awake while the rest took a turn resting. If that didn't work, then they were in deep trouble.

chapter
—17—

Owl Claw had watched closely since these strangers entered his home country. Ate Two Rabbits had given him food for thought, and he had quietly kept an eye on that skinny hunter as he settled down for the first night camp, while his people kept their gazes upon these newcomers.

There had been no fault with any of his people as they crept into that sleeping camp. The passing of the Yaqui, the Ute, the Pawnee made the old Digger smile, knowing that almost at their feet lay those who had gone to steal the riches these alien people possessed.

Even the sharpest senses would miss the Real People; indeed, to creep up on a lizard or a snake and catch it with one's hands required both subtlety and speed. Only another of his kind could catch the Paiute if he did not intend to be caught.

He was too old, too stiff to slip on his belly through a camp of armed men, but he knew just where each of his kinsmen would go and what they would do when they arrived. His years of leading the concerted grasshopper or rabbit drives that combined the forces of many small groups had given him an understanding of how men thought and acted.

He had seen the woman-hunger in the eyes of Ate Two Rabbits for many seasons now, and he understood what that one intended to steal. If he had been the one to go, he also would have chosen the man-woman, and he knew that his kinsman would take her.

That gave him a point on which to fix his gaze. Even with eyes clouded by age, the old Digger managed to focus on the distant piles of goods, the recumbent figures of the pale-haired man and the woman. That was where he had expected Ate Two Rabbits to appear, and he was not disappointed.

When the pale dot that was the woman's face disappeared, Owl Claw grunted softly. He had her, then. Soon they would come out of the camp silently, without being noticed by the watchful scouts, and then he would help his kinsman examine this very strange person.

He could see flickers of motion when the scouts passed on their rounds. Determining the thick clump of bushes toward which Ate Two Rabbits was moving, he also began creeping in that direction.

Before he could arrive there, somewhat more slowly than his kinsman, he heard a quiet sound. Death had entered the spot behind the bushes, to which the woman had been dragged. Whose death?

He smelled blood. Before he could move, he heard a yell of warning from the woman, and then everything blurred into confusion. The beautiful, precise movements of the Paiute raiders were disrupted as sleepers woke and caught the stealthy intruders all but on top of them, engaged in working free targeted weapons and furs and pots and knives.

Owl Claw would have killed those who tried to take the scanty food that was now all he could catch. He would have understood if those aliens had killed the men they caught, but that was not what they did. Only Ate Two Rabbits died that night, and Owl Claw understood that; the woman had defended herself, as was anyone's right. That death had been earned.

Still, they must not allow this treasure of animal flesh and metal goods to escape without further tries at getting more into the hands of his people. Retreating into the concealment of the swampy country, Owl Claw gathered his disturbed people together and heard their stories.

While they were not the equals of his kind at detecting intruders in the night, it was plain that those pale skins were tough and skilled with weapons. More subtlety was going to be needed. They must follow, learning more about this tricky prey. The next day he led, and all his people fit to travel followed as the strangers moved along the river very quickly on their long-legged beasts.

Exhaustion threatened to halt the excursion. Some of those who were injured or sick dropped out entirely. Yet as they went, others of their kind joined them, until at last many, many double hands of warriors dogged the heels of the travelers. As many as had ever combined their efforts in one of the annual game drives now followed Owl Claw on the trail of the strangers.

The camps those people chose were very difficult to approach, and Owl Claw bided his time. But his nephew, Six Rats by the Tail, was young and impetuous. He tried to catch and kill a horse that broke free from the bunch at the end of the line of riders.

The pale skin who followed after the horse aimed his long weapon at the young man. The explosion that followed deafened Owl Claw and most of those with him. Echoes reverberated up and down the river canyon like the ghosts of thunder as their fellow tribesman jerked backward and fell.

When they looked again, Six Rats lay still on the dung-studded trail, and the horse was taken to rejoin the others. There was a great red hole in the boy's chest, and his blood pooled about him on the grit of the riverbank. Six Rats by the Tail, the most promising, the bravest, the most intelligent of the young Paiutes, was dead.

When that became plain to Owl Claw, the old man looked about at his companions. "We will fight them," he said. "We will kill them all." There was no objection from any of his stunned companions.

From that point onward, they made certain their quarry could not hear or see or smell them. They watched as the camps were made, always in places that prevented surprise attacks. But the Paiute were a patient people, used to deprivation that would have destroyed lesser men.

On they went, out of the canyon, never slowing their

determined pursuit. In the flatter country beyond the mouth of the canyon, they saw the camp where their prey would spend the night.

As he traveled, the old man felt inside his heart for a sign, for a dream, for a vision. His old legs aching with effort, his belly lank for lack of food, he waited, and at last it came. He knew the way, and it lived inside him as he watched his people circle the camp of his quarry.

Owl Claw waited until the fires were out, except for the great one that burned all night, fed by dead wood brought from the river. Then he stood and stepped forth from the circle of his people. He took his wooden lance and a chunk of wood he had brought from a dead cottonwood beside the stream.

He began to pound on it, the beat slow and steady as a gigantic heart. Soon the others with him took up the rhythm, *beat*-beat, *beat*-beat, until the very soil beneath their bare feet throbbed with the sound. The rhythm caught at his mind, echoed his pulse, and filled him with purpose.

Much to Owl Claw's pleasure, those in the camp rose from their blankets. No one would rest tonight, he was determined. Even armed as they were, if the white men were weary, it must be easier to defeat them. The People needed no rest, if there was something to gain. They walked without food or sleep until they achieved their goals. The sleepless night would trouble those in the camp, but it would be nothing to his kind.

He raised his withered face to the sky, where the waning moon had not yet risen. Stars greeted him, flickering in the distance, as he shouted, "You have killed my nephew. Now we will kill you!"

They would not understand his words, he felt, but they could not mistake his meaning.

The thudding of the makeshift wooden drums filled the night, rolling across the flat country to echo faintly from the distant ridges to the west and north. Owl Claw was almost able to sleep while he drummed, so automatic did the effort become. His eyes closed from time to time, as he was lulled by the steady beat.

The moon rose, red and misshapen, and began to cross the sky. The white men in their camp kept their fire high, although they must be using dung for fuel, the old man thought. Out there in the open there was nothing to burn, and they could not have carried enough wood to keep it burning so hotly for so long.

The distant firelight sparked off those long weapon-tubes, gleaming also on the pale faces of watchers in the camp. Owl Claw could feel the tension growing among his enemies. They would learn that no one killed the nephew of Owl Claw without paying a dreadful price.

The drumming went on and on and a paleness in the east marked the approach of dawn. It swallowed the sick moon at last, and when the warm light touched the faces of the ridges, the old man was ready.

He had worked it out carefully, after thinking hard about the terrible boom of the stick, the big hole in Six Rats's chest, the quickness of the mounted men. It would not be wise for his people to take their weapons into their hands and charge the encampment. No, he was an older and a wiser man than that.

In his thoughts he could see his people falling before that artificial thunder, their blood draining into the dust as his nephew's had done. There were too few of his kind to waste their lives in such a way. There were more intelligent tactics, and he had found one, he was sure.

All through that night of drumming, his mind had been busy, even as his eyes rested. Inside his head he saw the way the white men dealt with the tribes traveling with them. They spoke together without hostility. If they would agree to speak with his people inside that camp, it would take his warriors within the defenses. Once there, the thing would be easy.

At hand-to-hand combat there was no one wirier or more tricky than one of his Paiute people, the old warrior knew. So when the camp had roused and its people were busy packing up their gear, he gestured to One Mouse, who was brother to Ate Two Rabbits and a wise man in his own right.

"We will go and speak with these strangers," Claw said, watching the man from the corners of his eyes. "We will offer to guide them through our country. All of our people will come into their camp together. What do you think?"

One Mouse looked down, thinking. Then he looked up into Claw's eyes, and a spark of understanding sprang between them. "We will be as peaceful as ants in a dunghill," Mouse said. "And I will go with you to speak with them. Those who guide them understand Sign, for I have seen them use hand talk among themselves."

The two nodded agreement. Then Claw spoke of his plan to the others, before finally gesturing for the rest to remain in place while he and One Mouse walked with great dignity toward the watching white men.

Before they reached the edge of the camp, the smallest of the men there came forward to meet them. Beside him was the Ute, and behind them came the strange warrior-woman who had killed Ate Two Rabbits.

When they came face-to-face, Claw gestured for all to sit, for no Digger stood when he could sit or sat when he could lie at full length. The conservation of energy was a fine art among his kind. It was a matter of wonder to him that these strangers moved about so much when there was no necessity for it.

In a rough circle, he and Mouse, the small man, and his two red-skinned people sat cross-legged, solemn and alert. The Ute raised his hand in the sign of peace. Knowing full well that he was lying, Owl returned the gesture. Then he got down to business.

He was aware, even as he asked to come into the camp and talk with the white travelers, that the woman was following his sign with complete attention. He could feel her gaze on him, even without looking toward her, and her intentness filled him with unease. She alone of these people was a totally unknown quantity.

But he finished his mission, and the Ute nodded abruptly before turning to talk the strange tongue of the white man. It was not understandable to Owl Claw's ears, but he watched the little man's face closely and knew that he understood what had been asked.

Good. Perhaps there would be an easy way to take what these people had and to avenge his nephew's death.

It was better to lose a few warriors than many. If they had to kill all these who were not truly human, then so be it, for they had no value other than their goods. They were not, after all, the true and genuine People.

Claw rose and held up his hand. Then he turned with great dignity and moved back toward his waiting warriors.

chapter
—18—

Second Son had watched the Diggers even more closely since the midnight kidnap attempt. Some sense she had never known before seemed to warn her that there was danger there, even though they looked so weak and ill-armed. After that night, she kept a sharp eye on the back trail, for she knew that those hungry people would never stop until it was proven to them, possibly through blood and death, that they could not take what the travelers possessed.

She understood their thinking, for in a much less compelling manner it was the way her own people lived. Goods were for the taking, being unimportant except for survival value. The white man's strange fixation upon keeping what he considered his had amused her, once she understood it. Even Cleve, who was becoming more Cheyenne than white man, still had something of that element in his heart.

She said little, except to Yellow Hair, but she knew that the Diggers were behind them as they rode and walked and camped and rode again. And when they cleared the canyon and camped in open country, she knew that before long the party would have a circle of Diggers around them.

Again, this was the way her own people would have acted, given such terrible need. Those who had food or blankets, among most of the tribes she knew, shared what they possessed with those who had nothing. If any starved, they all starved together. With white men it seemed to be different.

Before going to rest, she approached Walters, who sat on a low rock beside the cookfire, making small marks in the little book he carried. He looked up as she came near and nodded for her to sit on an adjacent stone.

"Looks as if you've got a word to say," he said, putting the book into the pouch slung about his shoulder. "I been wondering what you might think of those folks out there." He nodded toward the dim shapes ringing the camp.

"They will try to get our horses to eat and our blankets and weapons to use or to admire," she said. "But you know this. I have watched as they settled into place, and I can point to their leader. That very old one, whose hair shines white, is their wise man."

"The boss, eh?" Walters stared toward the spot where the old man had last been seen.

She shook her head, making her eagle feathers flap against her neck. "No. Our kind do not have such things, as white men understand that. But they do respect those who have lived long and learned much. They will take his advice, though he could not order them to do anything they disliked doing.

"They respect him. I have been watching as men go to him and talk and then go away again to their own places in the circle. It is he who will realize—it may be that he already has—that they cannot hope to overcome us by attacking openly, over a distance. He has seen the blood of the man Toosh killed. He now understands what guns can do."

The small man's eyes narrowed, and he nodded slowly, as if digesting her words. "So what will this wise man decide to do?" he asked, though she suspected that he had already figured that for himself.

"He will try to negotiate with us. Possibly he will try to trade something they have for something we have, though it should be obvious that is not possible. Or they may try to come and talk with us, smoke with us, bringing enough of their people into this camp to overcome us, once they are in our midst."

Walters nodded again. "Pretty much my own thinking," he said. "If he asks to parley, you want to come with the Ute and me? You read sign, and you talk a lot better English than Quiet Coyote. I'd be glad to have you along to read 'em, if nothing else."

"I will come," she said, rising. As she returned to the sleeping place she thought about what might happen tomorrow. She could not believe that the Diggers would be so unintelligent as to attack openly, even by night, but she wondered what move they would make when their plan did not work. Morning was not the time she would have chosen to talk with the Paiute, after that night of drumming. Still, if Walters wanted to parley instead of moving his people out immediately through the circle of waiting men, that was his concern.

She followed Walters and the Ute as the sun rose, staying behind them, watching the faces of the two men who were approaching the camp. That old one was a thinker, she could see from his high brow and the wrinkles about his eyes.

He would believe, knowing nothing of white men's devious ways, that his thoughts were as secret from these strangers as they were from his own kind. She felt a bit sorry for him as she settled into the circle, facing him.

There had been a time when she, too, had felt that the ways of her people were the ways of the world. First the Oglala, then the Pawnee, and lastly the white men's Rendezvous had taught her that what one person could plan, another could guess and circumvent. No, the old man, deceived because he had lived his life among those of his own kind, would be disappointed to find his clever plan useless.

She sat silent, watching him, listening to the Ute's translations of the sign the Digger made. It went as she expected, and she could see the glint of satisfaction in the white-haired one's eyes when he turned at last to his waiting circle, now numbering a great many double hands of men.

When at last she moved toward their own camp with her companions, she knew the old one believed there was a chance to gain his goals. She said as much to Walters, who smiled. "Thought so myself," he said. "We're goin' to saddle up and get out of here before they can make another plan."

It happened quickly, after that, for the mountain men were fast and their Indian women and guides even faster than that. She had seen, among her people, an entire village alerted and on the move in the time it took for the sun to brighten behind the horizon, top the distant ridges, and reach across the lands to touch the place where the tipis had rested.

The Paiute stirred, rising in surprise as the travelers mounted. Second Son saw the white hair of the old man shine in the new sunlight as she kneed Shadow after the packhorses. Then the party was moving, heading out in a wedge that split the ring of Diggers neatly, letting everyone through with a minimum of fuss.

Behind them, as they galloped across the wide flat in the curve of the river, the Cheyenne heard a yell of fury. Rocks and lances flew, striking horses and riders but doing no damage. A lance sailed past her and touched the flank of Cleve's horse, ahead, but it had lost velocity and fell harmlessly to the ground.

She urged her mount to catch up with Cleve. He glanced aside and grinned, and she knew he had hoped for a battle. She felt a bit the same, but those skinny, unarmed warriors would not be an honorable match for people who were fit and well equipped.

• • •

Walters set a grueling pace after that; the Diggers, already weary and afoot, could not hope to keep pace with the mounted men. Even the past night of drumming had not kept the animals from resting, and the riders had let their bodies relax, even if they could not sleep.

They moved within sight of the river now, though not beside it. Instead of bearing south and west, the stream had curved to come from the north and west, and Second Son saw that Walters was writing often in his small book, as if noting the route they took and making sketches of landmarks. Mapmaking was one of the white man's skills that she found very useful and intelligent.

Emerging from a ravine one evening many camps later, Second Son saw, to her surprise, a spiky line of snow-capped heights lying along the horizon. Those were not the familiar contours of the Rockies, high and steep, but far less abrupt. These peaks were like knives thrust into the sky, angled and sheer and, even at such a distance, formidable.

After the party halted for the night, Cleve helped her to set up their camp. He kept gazing off toward the peaks, now black silhouettes against the blazing sunset.

"That's the kind of place where Smith got snowed in. Lost men and horses. It looks like a mighty nasty place to cross," he said. "I hope we're in time to make it before the real snows begin."

She nodded. At those heights, winter came far earlier than it did in the lower country. Even now, just past the end of a particularly hot, dry summer, the snow seemed thick and undisturbed. There would come no thaw up there, she thought. New snowfall would simply thicken the pack already in place.

She wondered what passes might cut across those heights—or was there a way that avoided the highest part of the range? From the look of those distant mountains, any pass they found would be a high one, and even at this time of year they might well find new snow falling. Clouds drifted across the jagged teeth, even now, and she shivered.

That night passed peacefully, except for distant howls of coyotes and the soft wing beats of hunting owls. When Second Son rose the next morning, she found her legs cramping. That had happened with Billy-Wolf, too, she recalled, but she worked the hard muscles with both hands until they softened. Her interior unease had become so familiar that she no longer heeded it.

Cleve came with the packhorses and looked down. "Problems?" he asked.

She shook her head. "Nothing that is not expected. I will be well, Yellow Hair. White men worry too much about natural things like dying and being born."

But when they rode out of camp and the mountains sank behind nearer ridges, she felt strange, queasy, almost faint, which was a thing she had never before experienced in her entire life. She took her place in line just behind the Ute Woman, with Cleve following their string of packhorses behind her.

Two Big Feet looked back and saw her. The black eyes showed no emotion, though the woman nodded, a quick jerk of the chin.

The country seemed endless, the mountains beyond invisible in the long stretches of broken land, then looming at the end of flatter reaches, as if taunting those who were trying to come to their foothills.

But mountains were deceptive, the Cheyenne knew. They looked near, but one could journey for days without seeming to get any closer. Then, with breathtaking suddenness, there they would be, looming over those who approached them like giant spirits, too preoccupied with matters of sky and wind and weather to notice tiny men who crept at their feet.

So it was with the Sierras. The Yaqui had traveled in that direction before, with others of his kind, on some unknown mission. He knew a pass, he told Walters, in Second Son's presence, that could be used, though it would not be an easy one.

"The bones of many travelers lie beneath the snows, for I have spoken with those tribes living beyond," the man said in passable Spanish. Second Son had made it a point to learn that tongue, once she began meeting Mexicans at Rendezvous, so she often translated between the Yaqui and Walters.

"We will approach so. . . ." He drew a series of dots into the dust between the squatting travelers. "Here we follow the mountains north. . . ." He piled neat clumps of sand to demonstrate, and it looked to Second Son as if that in itself was going to be a long journey, beneath the very shoulder of the range.

But the Yaqui was busy again, marking a twisting groove into the upper reaches of his tiny model. "There we can cross, if we have good fortune. I have passed that way and returned alive. It can be done."

When she finished her translation, Walters looked thoughtfully at the forbidding towers of stone rising above their route. "Not an easy trip, I take it," he said, his tone wry. "But we're a tough bunch of coots, and that's no lie."

He looked into the scout's dark eyes. "Good work, Cucha. You lead and we'll follow."

Second Son didn't need to translate that, for the Yaqui understood quite a bit more English than he could twist around his tongue. He nodded and sank onto his heels, letting the white men chew over this chunk of information he had just fed them.

Her work done, Second Son felt a sudden need to rest. She had seldom thought, in her years as a man, of the hardship being pregnant might work upon the women of her people. Her first pregnancy had been relatively easy, for they had been settled into a permanent camp before she got very heavy.

This time she felt subtly uneasy, as if something were not quite right inside her body. It was still early—it had been only two moons since Cleve had asked if she carried a child, so now it was only about three in all. Yet she felt as if her ankles were already trying to swell, her belly to feel waterlogged.

No, something was very wrong; she shivered to think how pained Cleve would be if she died here so far from their son and her people. She unrolled the sleeping blankets and lay flat, breathing deeply and trying to relax her taut muscles. The feeling eased somewhat, and she sighed. Perhaps it was only a temporary problem that would solve itself.

There came a polite cough, and she opened her eyes. Two Big Feet was in the act of sinking onto the pile of blankets beside the sleeping place. The woman's face was expressionless, but her eyes were fixed on Second Son's.

"You carry baby." It was not a question.

The Cheyenne nodded. "Almost three moons now," she

said. "But something is not right with me. It is different from before."

"All are not the same," the Ute said. "I have borne four, and each was different. You are sick?"

"Not really sick," Second Son replied. "More uneasy. Something seems to cry a warning inside."

The big woman stared at her large feet, as if thinking hard. When she looked up, she said, "You are not like any woman I know, yet you do not look down upon those who are the wives of the other men. You hunt. You killed the Paiute when he took you away, but you also are quiet and you do not push arrogantly as young warriors are apt to do."

Second Son wondered what her point might be, but the woman went on.

"I have brought many babies. Few women have died in my hands and even fewer infants. I will tend you, if you will let me. You did not shame me before my man. The other women do not matter, and I have forgotten our quarrel."

Relieved, Second Son nodded. "I will be glad to have a woman of experience at my side," she said, "if anything goes wrong as we travel. And if we arrive together at the Great Water, then I will be happy to have you with me when the child is born."

Two Big Feet rose and looked down at her. It was as if a treetop had deigned to notice a person walking beneath, yet her eyes were warm now, not hostile. But she said nothing more, simply turned toward her own campsite toward which her husband was making his way.

The conference had broken up. Cleve was coming. Second Son felt inside herself, but the momentary unease had quieted. Perhaps feeling that someone who knew about such matters was nearby had calmed her body and her mind.

That was good. Tomorrow they would begin the long trek toward the pass that would take them beyond the mountains that rose so near the journey's end.

chapter

19

The long journey through totally unfamiliar country had been an experience he would not have missed, Cleve thought. And now this new obstacle, this range that should have been simply another batch of mountains to cross but was so much more, filled him with excitement.

Those snowy upthrusts, often with their heads filmed with cloud, seemed somehow both arrogant and frightening, and it had been a long while since anything scared him. He felt both anticipation and awe as the party traveled toward the pass.

Cucha insisted that was the only good way for getting such a large group of men and horses over the heights. Yet the closer the group came, the more difficult the range seemed. Already the film of cloud was thicker, darker, more forbidding.

If it had not been for his concern about his wife, Cleve would have wished for storms and snows and thunders to accompany the passage they faced. However, though Second Son said nothing and did not allow her discomfort to show to anyone, he still had a sense that all was not well with her.

The quiet attentiveness of the big Ute woman told him that she, too, was concerned. That strange friendship now growing between Second Son and Two Big Feet had at first amused Cleve, though he was glad of it. A woman in her condition needed a female friend, he thought.

At last, one evening while the stewpot simmered, he approached Quiet Coyote and squatted beside the tiny fire his woman had kindled near their sleeping spot. The Ute glanced from the corners of his eyes, obviously wondering what Bennett wanted of him.

Cleve found it difficult to form his wish into words, but at last he said, "Coyote, I wish to speak to your woman. My own woman may have a trouble, and I need the words of one who understands such things. Would you object if I ask Two Big Feet some questions?"

The Ute pushed a stick of wood into the coals, as if thinking. Then he said, "Often women are wise. They think about things men do not understand. Two Big Feet is strong thinker. You will speak."

Reassured, Cleve turned to find those two large feet

planted just behind him. "Your woman—you wish to talk about?" asked the Ute.

"I do," said Cleve. "If you will sit with me on these rocks so that we do not trouble your man, I would like to ask you some questions."

She nodded and led the way to the gritty slabs. Once she was solidly plopped onto the stone, she looked at him questioningly. She didn't intend to give him any help, Cleve saw at once, but he didn't really blame her. Women among this group got very little help and less sympathy.

"My wife does not speak of it," he began carefully, "but I think she is not well. The child she carries—do you know if it is going as it should? I see you ride beside her, and sometimes you speak. Perhaps she has told you."

The big woman cocked her head, studying him with care. When she was satisfied, she leaned forward. "Second Son feel strangeness inside. She sometimes sick, sometimes very weak. She does not let show."

She paused for a long moment, as if wondering how much to tell this ignorant male. Then she sighed and continued, "I promise to stay beside her, help if there is trouble. Maybe so, I deliver the child when is time. I watch her close. See her color turn yellow, her body swell. Something not natural."

Cleve felt his heart give a dismal thud, and as if she saw that in his face, the woman became more open. She almost smiled as she said, "No be afraid. Sometimes this happen, and child is born early. Such time, it does not live, but mother able to bear more. Can be bad, but maybe so not happen if take care."

"Riding all over the confounded country can't be good for her," he muttered. "I should've taken her home a way back before we reached the Humboldt Sink. But she said she'd go anyway, so what could I do?"

"That is not woman you take away against her will," Two Big Feet agreed. "Digger found that out. He died for it. I watch her close. If she show blood or bad pain, come find me." She rose with great dignity and moved toward her campfire.

She did not look back, and Cleve stared after her, a bit awed at the authority this woman could call upon, given the opportunity. It might be, he thought, that all the Indian women could be Second Sons, if they chose.

A startling thought came to him. Could white women do the same, if they were not taught to keep to their houses and gardens? He had seen his mother take rifle in hand more than once when trouble with Indians or neighbors threatened her home. His sister-in-law lacked nothing in courage and skill when the need for it came around. Why did his people seem so set upon making their women weaklings? But that was too hard a question, and he pushed it from his mind as he went back to his bedroll and lay down beside his wife.

Second Son was near sleep, yet she murmured as he touched her shoulder and nestled closer to him. He put an arm about her, feeling an unaccustomed thinness in her body.

The Ute was right. There was something wrong, and he could only hope that nothing terrible would happen to her before they reached the Spanish enclave about which Smith had spoken.

The days passed, and the Sierras now were so near that the furring of trees on the steep slopes was visible. Dark ravines cut the lower areas and marked the snowy heights with purple.

The Yaqui seemed to be heading straight into an impassable place, but Bennett knew this had to be the way. Walters would certainly not go blindly into unnecessary danger, for he was, above all else, a careful planner.

They came to the foothills, and the heights were invisible most of the time, hidden by the nearer hills and the increasing numbers of trees. A stream watered the way now, with incredible numbers of birds and small animals flourishing amid the well-watered growth.

Second Son seemed to forget her discomfort as she ranged aside with her bow and brought back rabbits and woodchucks, antelope and grouse. They used their own pot, instead of partaking of the communal stew, while moving along this rich country, for she also found wild plants that provided leaves and roots to flavor their food.

Cleve almost forgot his worry as they traveled, marveling at the strange kinds of birds that thronged in the treetops. The waters were alive with ducks and swans as well, and everyone fattened as they moved inexorably toward the waiting range.

The tense lines about Second Son's eyes eased, and Cleve felt his spirits lift. With the enthusiasm of a boy, he rode over the hills with Walters or Douglas, the Ute or the Yaqui, scouting for tribes that might live there.

"The Tubatu and the Kitane live near. I meet them before," said Cucha. "We should meet some of their people here, for they come late in year to gather last supply of food."

Before they reached the first steep slopes of the mountains, Cleve realized how true that was. He had ridden onto a ridge above the line of riders, and he sat amid the trees and rocks, gazing at the land beyond. He saw movement amid the thick growth downslope, and at once he dismounted. Dropping flat, he gave the birdcall that told Second Son to alert the leaders below.

In the distance, small shapes slipped through the brush and out of sight. Not even a bird rose to warn of their passing, and he knew that without his Cheyenne training he might have missed these other travelers entirely.

They might well be those Tubatu or Kitane that Cucha had mentioned, but he had no idea if they would react in a friendly manner to a yellow-haired white man. He crept back down toward his own party and settled his horse in a patch of brush.

When he topped the ridge again, he was lying flat, concealed in the berry bushes that now hung heavy with ripening fruit. A camp-robber jay settled onto the branch above his head and began pecking at the purplish berries.

He felt a sudden breath of air stir past his ear and turned to see Cucha behind him, silent as a mole, almost invisible as he slid through the stripes of sun and shadow to join him. Cleve pointed downward toward the point at which he thought the file of walkers might emerge from the wrinkle of land into which they had disappeared.

"There, I think," he whispered.

The Yaqui's dark eyes focused on the distant dot that was a break in the vegetation. His aquiline nose seemed to sharpen as he leaned forward like a dog scenting game. After a moment a quiver in the bushes signaled the movements of something among them.

Cleve wondered, watching Cucha, what the Yaqui was thinking—why, indeed, the man had agreed to accompany this group westward. His people lived to the south, far from here, though he never referred to family or tribe. Had he fallen afoul of the Spaniards who controlled his native lands?

Then the trapper's own gaze caught the first bronze dot that was a face rising amid the dusty green. One . . . two . . . three . . . four figures came up the slope, out of that runnel they had followed.

Bennett could almost feel the tension in the Yaqui's gaze as he concentrated upon those distant men. Then he rose slowly to his full height and sent a whistle into the air—a hunting hawk, circling above, would have answered it.

Trusting to Cucha's lead, Cleve rose, too, though he felt terribly exposed on the ridge. He knew very well that only the sharpest eye, knowing where to look, could have picked him out at such a distance, dwarfed by the rocks and trees about him. Yet always he hated to stand out against the skyline when strangers were within range. He had been hunted by too many enemies, over the years, to feel comfortable doing that.

The travelers below paused and at once they were invisible, melting into the foliage of the hillside. Cucha gestured for Cleve to wait in place, and obediently Bennett sank onto his heels in the shade of a thicket. He watched the short, square-shouldered shape move down the hill.

If the Utes had impressed him, the Yaqui had, during this stressful journey, filled him with awe. Silent as a stone, most of the time, the man seemed to smell and taste and feel the country around them.

He was afraid of nothing, as he had proved by going ahead of the party in the roughest country where no path seemed to exist. He had scaled impossible cliffs to spy out the countryside, leaving behind any weapon except his knife. He seemed to court death, Cleve had decided, which made him wonder if some terrible thing in his past drove the man.

Whatever the cause, he was constantly risking his neck, scouting out dangers that were only a feeling in the gut, invisible to the eye. Now he was walking freely to meet people who might well greet him with a flurry of arrows or a knife in the gut.

Cleve felt that he might have argued against staying behind, but somewhat to his shame, he was also glad the Yaqui had left him in place. That was an entirely new kind of Indian, down there.

Cucha was now within hailing distance of the three. Cleve could hear the faint sound of a voice, answered by another, but even if he had understood the language, he could not have distinguished words. Hands moved, telling him that language had broken down and Sign was filling its gaps.

After some time Cucha turned back and signaled for him to bring Walters, the sign for whom was a hand held at shoulder level. That always amused Bennett, for it referred to the leader's short stature.

Chuckling, he slid back over the ridge to his mount and rode down toward a spot at which he would probably intersect the line of riders. The sun was past the zenith by the time he returned with Walters, the Ute, and Beeville, leaving Freeman Douglas to lead the group forward.

When they came to the top of the ridge, Cucha was crouched in the thicket where Cleve had waited. With him were three small, wiry men, their faces still and waiting, their hands very near their knife slings.

Leaving their horses downslope to graze, Cleve led his companions upward and Cucha rose to meet them. The Indians with him rose, too, seemingly calm and controlled, but Cleve felt a certain tension about them, as if they were poised for flight at any hostile move.

He didn't blame them at all. In this situation he probably would never have consented to meet with a lot of strangers with odd weapons and alien coloring, no matter who asked him to.

But they remained dignified as they greeted these newcomers, gesturing with all the aplomb of hosts to guests for all to sit cross-legged in the shade for this talk. The sign for peace passed around the circle with suitable deliberateness.

Walters drew forth a pipe he had traded for among the Dakotah, filling it slowly from the decorated pouch of tobacco he carried. There was no fire to light it, but he passed it solemnly around the circle, and the Indians seemed to understand and approve the ritual.

Then Quiet Coyote spoke a couple of words in a questioning tone, and the oldest of the three strangers looked surprised and answered him. Cleve leaned back against a chunk of rock, satisfied that there was going to be communication. In this country, that was a damn good beginning.

chapter 20

Walters had sweated every mile of the journey, knowing that each moment of delay meant the loss of precious days. On the merciless passes of the Sierras, the snows would not wait; he had listened with close attention to Smith's account of his terrible time there, and it was a warning he could not ignore. He did not intend to lead either his men or himself to such a chilly death.

The Yaqui had made that crossing more than once, and he was not totally reassuring as to the chance of getting so many people and horses over the chosen pass, if they arrived after the big snows began on the heights. Sometimes those came while summer still baked the lowlands, and September, which was now passing quickly, was very late to make the attempt.

When Bennett came down the ridge and told Malachi they had found local Indians who would talk, he hoped that they would give good advice as to his approach to the mountains. Only those who lived in this country and knew the Sierras, season by season, could give knowledgeable reports concerning conditions in this current year.

The three short, wiry Tubani who waited were no taller than he, which was somehow comforting. They had flat, emotionless faces, but in their eyes he read great curiosity about his people and his equipment. Even as he sat across from the trio, Malachi decided that if they provided useful information, he would reward them with good steel knives from the supply of possible gifts he had brought.

Luckily the Ute understood much of their tongue and was able to communicate with them. Yet, as the dialogue went forward, Walters felt his heart drop.

"The snows have begun. Kesho and his people come down two hand of days past. Snow right behind them. They hunt the high country for great sheep of the mountains, and the first storm almost catch them. Kesho say many bones of his people lie up there. Passes they are treacherous and often deceive even the most skillful."

Of course, it took longer to get that information from Kesho, and Quiet Coyote's translations required much time and effort. Yet when Walters had absorbed what was said, that was the gist of it.

"Then it is too late to make the crossing here?" he asked.

Quiet Coyote spoke to the leader, using Sign when his vocabulary failed him. When he turned, he looked thoughtful. "Is another pass; little river come down from the mountain, cut a ravine into side. Man, perhaps horse, too, can pass that way. Snow come there later than here. Not so deep, maybe so."

Walters gestured for a pause and turned to the Yaqui. "Cucha, do you know of this other pass?" he asked.

The Yaqui nodded once, decisively. "Is very bad for horse," he said. "Very hard. But is lower than here. Maybe so we make it, maybe so not."

Malachi turned back to Quiet Coyote. "Do these men think it is not snowed deeply there yet?"

There was another bout of language and Sign, and when the Ute was confident of the meaning, he looked a bit more cheerful. "They say it snow up there anytime. But not yet this season, not so much. But do not go this way here. That is what they tell me."

Walters nodded, feeling very fortunate that Cleve had spotted these hunters before they returned to their winter camp. "Tell them I will give them good knives, Coyote. I brought some things in my pack. Tell them to wait for a bit until Cucha can bring the gifts I have for them."

As the Ute translated Walters saw the eyes of Kesho widen minimally. But the Indian's face did not change while Malachi waited for the Yaqui.

When the pack arrived, Walters made a long job of opening it and taking out the chosen gifts. First came a good steel knife in a leather sheath. Kesho's face almost changed expression when Malachi handed it over to him with a gesture of thanks.

Two more knives emerged from the parfleche bag, and

the other Tubani began to smile—or at least as much of a smile as their narrow-lipped mouths could manage. They were obviously much younger than their leader and had not yet learned the iron control that Kesho demonstrated so completely.

When Walters rose and held up his hand in the peace sign, Kesho returned the gesture. Then he turned, slipped away down the slope, and was gone from sight, with his two companions, as if he had never existed.

Cleve Bennett took the twig he was chewing from between his teeth. "I think we lucked out, finding those people right here, right now, before we started up that damn mountain. Looks as if we're going to have to take that other pass, if we can find it."

"Cucha know the way," the Yaqui said. "Not take it first. Too hard, too long, too bad for horse. Now must take. Get across, maybe so."

"That's got to be the way, whether we like it or not. We can't risk our lives and our animals in snow that's already too deep to travel through." Walters gestured to the others and moved down the other side of the ridge toward the browsing horses.

"I think I'll send you, Cleve, and the Yaqui to scout out the way ahead. I'll bring on the rest as fast as we can move, and by the time we find that little river, you may know enough to leave a sign to guide us. That all right with you?"

Cleve mounted his stallion and looked away across the hills toward the towering peaks. "Fine with me. Just you watch out for Second Son. She's pregnant, and things aren't going quite right."

That came as something of a shock to Walters. He had

taken the Cheyenne at her own valuation, as a warrior and hunter, and it had not occurred to him to think that she was also Bennett's wife. Wives got pregnant, and usually at inconvenient times. Why should this one be any different?

"Will do," he said. He followed the Ute down the slope, angling toward the line of march the party should be following. By now it was late afternoon, and when he drew abreast of Beeville at the head of the riders, he asked, "Campsite been located yet?"

Beeville pointed forward. "The Pawnee's gone ahead to scout out a good spot. What'd you find out up there?"

"That we can't use the easy route. Snowed in already, the Indians say. But they told us about another one, harder but not deep in snow yet. The Yaqui knows the way, and I'm sending him and Bennett ahead tomorrow to find our path. That all right with you?"

Seldom did Beeville offer advice, and almost never did Walters ask for his opinion. He'd been hired to run this operation, and that was that. But he felt obscurely uneasy about this change of plans, and when Beeville nodded, it was reassurance that he needed.

The Pawnee returned before dark and led the weary riders to a meadow beside a creek. There was abundant grass for the animals, plenty of deadfall from the willows and cottonwoods for camp and cookfires, and it was sheltered from the wind, which was already blowing cold at those altitudes.

After supper, Walters huddled with Bennett, Second Son, the Ute, the Yaqui, and Beeville, drawing new maps, as well as they could manage, of the route they must take. Remembering Kesho's directions with complete accuracy, Quiet Coyote quoted them, and Malachi translated his words into marks in his notebook.

Then the group bent over a patch of dry ground, using twigs and finger marks to form a map. "Put rock here," said Coyote. "That big hill, he say, with rock sit on top. You turn south there, round bottom of hill. Go one day's march—that maybe half day's ride. Those men, they go fast, even when walk."

Cleve was rubbing his chin as he studied the map. "All right, we go south, following the foot of that big hill. Then which direction and for how long?"

Coyote thought for a moment, obviously translating Kesho's words inside his head. "Two day to south, angle toward mountains. You find river soon, then. Not big—shallow, with many tree. Then follow up.

"Easy after that, until you get to deep ravine. Then you be careful. Much bad place."

Walters looked across the map at Second Son. She was bent over the drawing, staring down, and he felt sure that she would have gone with her husband if she had been in good health. He felt obscurely sorry for her when she straightened, pulled her loose robe about her, and glanced aside at her husband.

Bennett pulled from his pouch a square of deerhide. Then, taking great care, he sketched a copy of their makeshift map onto it with a charred twig, digging the charcoal into the hide so that even if it smeared, the line would still be legible.

"I'll go before light," the blond man said. "Cucha and I will mark trees or put rock signs along the way so you can follow easily.

"If we can, we'll come back to guide you through, but

don't worry if we don't make it. I've no idea at all how long this will take or what we'll find when we get up high. Could be there's been snow since Kesho and his hunters were there. We'll put warnings where you'll see 'em, if there's need."

Walters nodded. Of all his people, he felt most confident that Bennett would find the best and fastest way. Others might be better trackers or hunters, but Bennett had intelligence that was capable of reading situations and making the right decisions.

He'd seen that trait in the man on this long road they had traveled together, as well as earlier in their chance encounters. The success of his entire expedition might hang on just that ability.

chapter 21

Cleve had become weary of traveling among so many people. His life, since he left his Missouri home, had been mainly solitary, except for his family and occasional friends. Even those came seldom and didn't remain for long, because every trapper followed a timetable dictated by the seasons and the habits of the beaver. Most tended to be loners, and he was no exception.

That freedom was what he had wanted, and its disruption was, he found, irritating. For almost two months he had traveled in company with forty or fifty people he hardly knew and didn't care about one way or the other.

Now, heading out through the sharp, clean air of predawn, he felt as if he had been freed from some invisible yoke. His only regret was that Second Son did not ride beside him. That would have made this an adventure, instead of an ordinary mission.

He set aside the thought, for he knew he must not allow his worry about her to distract him from this venture. If the entire party was to survive, he and Cucha had to find a way through those staggering heights. That would not be easy.

It took most of the day to climb out of the hills near the first slopes of the Sierras. The big hill the Ute had told about, topped by a giant rock, stood out against the sky boldly. In the late evening, before camping for the night, Cleve and the Yaqui had traveled quite a distance around its foot, going up and down ravines gouged into its stony sides. It was not easy going, and often they marked out better routes for those who came behind them.

Antelope fled before them. Birds called harshly from the adjacent mountainside, and a wolf howled on some distant height. There was no sign of another human being, except for Cucha, and the Yaqui was so quiet that he might not have been there at all.

They found a sheltered spot just before full dark, at the foot of a ravine where a trickle of water ran from solid rock into a stony cup. The horses, freed of packs, whinnied with pleasure and began eating the sparse grass, now drying with approaching autumn. Concealed from any who might pass, it was an excellent place to camp.

They made no fire but chewed jerky and drank water from the spring. Then Cleve took the first watch. He knew that Cucha would be more alert than any white man in the small hours of the morning, and they needed no words to arrange their schedule. It was the logical way to do things, and both understood that.

The Yaqui did not seem contemptuous of the white men with whom he rode, but he was obviously aware of the whites' limitations as scouts and watchmen. He rolled at once into his blanket and was asleep before Cleve found a concealed spot, uncomfortable enough to keep him alert.

He leaned against the nubbly trunk of a tree, wondering what they would find above, in the pass. He shivered. Cold was a thing he endured without complaint, but it seemed to Cleve that he had not been really warm for most of his life, except when traveling in the blaze of the summer plains.

He thought of Second Son, curled against his back, warming his sleep. He sighed. She would be all right. He had to believe that, for life without her would be terrible to think about. His son would be with him, of course, and the Burning Heart people would always welcome him, but there would be a gap in his world that could not be filled.

He shook his head sharply to control his thoughts. Enough of that! He must think only of the night, the sounds of wind over bushes and rocks, of night birds and creaking insects. He had slept through having his wife removed from his side, and the disgrace of that would keep him awake for the rest of his watch.

The moon was dark now, and only multitudes of stars sparked the night. When he leaned away from his shelter, he could see past the mouth of the ravine, where the saw-toothed peaks of this range jagged upward, as if to eat the sky. A fanciful notion . . . he shook himself again.

Sleep dogged him, but he managed to stave it off, concentrating first on the near darkness, then on the peaks, on what he heard and what he smelled and what he felt in the blackness about him. When the Yaqui crawled silently toward him, he knew it at once, to his great pride.

He twittered like a sleepy bird. Cucha, very near now, grunted. "You sleep now. We go before day."

When Cleve woke, the first pewter shades were touching the edge of the sky, though it was still very dark. He rose quickly, rolled his blanket, and whistled for young Socks.

By the time he was mounted, Cucha was waiting for him, and he wondered if there was any way he could possibly make a faster start than the Yaqui. Probably not—even the most experienced trappers and explorers generally found their Indian guides waiting before they were ready to go.

They rode out of the ravine into the predawn darkness. Only the eastern edge of the sky was marked with light, but it was so dim and distant that it was of little help in picking safe footing for the horses. Cleve dismounted very soon and led his mount, watching closely. Breaking a horse's leg in a hole would put a stop to this expedition, for they could never cover enough distance afoot or riding and hitching.

Cucha was already afoot, moving ahead as surely as if he could see clearly. Maybe he could—Cleve had learned that necessity honed the senses of the plains and mountain people to an edge that no white man could hope to equal in less than a lifetime.

Following Cucha, he made better time as the two

worked their way over increasingly rough ground that now sloped upward more and more abruptly. From time to time they found their way barred by barriers of fallen rock or by steep-sided ravines, now dry but cut by spring runoff from the high snows. The footing was loose and shifty, except in the few places where the rockfalls had swept away the debris entirely.

The sky was light by the time they paused to chew a bit of jerky and rest the horses. Then it was possible to make better speed, though the foot of that terrible range was one that demanded the utmost care of those who traveled along it. Above there were occasional rumbles, and from time to time a scatter of rock came clattering down onto the toes of the heights.

Two days passed as they worked their way along the designated route, marking the way with slashes into the shaggy trunks of pines or by stacking flat rocks into small towers.

By the time they reached the river Quiet Coyote had mentioned, Cleve felt pretty well worn, but now their task was only just beginning. Keeping up with Cucha was a job for another Yaqui, he decided. The man never seemed to need rest.

The river itself wound among tumbles of rocks and clumps of willows, though at this time of year its waters were shallow, sometimes only pools studding the gravelly bed. Now turning gold, the willows shaded the bottom of the stream, and behind them rose larger trees, cottonwoods, and more pines. For a long distance the pair rode along the riverbed, the horses splashing the shallow water as if enjoying its coolness.

Then they came to the first rapids, too steep and rocky

to risk the horses in climbing. There they moved up onto the farther edge of the river's cut, where it seemed obvious that many kinds of game walked often on the way to drink from the pools below.

As Cleve led Socks upward he kept looking down over the uneven lip of stone that thrust out over the scanty flow of water below. Anything falling onto that sharp-toothed streambed would be chewed up and spat out downstream, he knew.

When a patch of ledge crumbled under Socks's weight, he pushed himself against the inner cliff and added his strength to the horse's efforts to keep its footing. For a moment he thought he and the stallion were lost, for the ledge kept slipping, but the pair of them managed to get the frantic hooves onto more solid stone just in time.

"Not a good way," he called out to Cucha, who was ahead, steadying his own mount. "You take a bunch of animals up this place, and it's going to come down in a tumble. Kill everybody, if you ask me."

Cucha pointed across the chasm. "You see there," he grated. "Other side better way, I think. Not see from down there, because animal use this one. Make think it good way. Now I see, I go back and make mark to go other side."

"Then why in hell did we come this way?" Cleve felt irritation rising inside him.

"Can't see good from there. From here, see mighty good. No break that side, so far. Plenty space to rest horse, sometime. Not many narrow place like here. They make it there. I go now. You watch step."

Cucha's tone was final, and Cleve knew better than to argue. He'd seen the Indian clam up and never speak a word for days on end when someone offended him. On this lonely ride, he'd miss having even the scanty conversation the Yaqui was willing to share. By the time Cucha got back from setting his sign in place, it had become downright lonely on that rocky trail.

He'd trust the man's sharp eyes to spot any danger along that opposite track, while keeping his own gaze fixed on the treacherous game trail at his feet. It wouldn't help anyone if he and Socks tumbled off that narrow trail and ended up as food for the buzzards.

After a night spent huddled on a small apron of rock extending over the trickle below, Cleve realized that they had been traveling the least difficult part of this trail. From that point on, the way grew steeper, more crooked, more treacherous. The other track, though wider and a lot less crumbly, didn't look a great deal better.

But he went forward doggedly, stepping in Cucha's tracks, longing for the earlier journey, when he could ride Socks instead of leading him. His moccasins, not new to begin with, wore thin, and he had to spend some of his needed resting time patching them with bits cut from his hide blanket.

Now the peaks loomed high over the ravine he followed, and it was plain to any eye that it had been snowing up there. At night a bitter wind swept down the river canyon, and the two travelers huddled together for warmth, wrapping both their blankets and their buffalo cloaks about them to hold in their body heat.

The horses were not happy, even with nose bags filled with grain brought for feeding them where there was no grass. The occasional rumble of a rock- or snow-slide higher up disturbed them, and their stamping and snuffling kept Cleve awake.

There was little rest to be found on the side of that mountain, he concluded, but when he stopped trying to keep his eyes closed, he dozed off at once. He had terrible dreams of a frosty-coated buffalo glaring at him from red-rimmed eyes.

They came out the next morning onto a shelf thrust out from the mountainside. Below them the ravine was now a slit ending in the glint of water far down in its shadow.

Shrugging his buffalo-hide cloak around him, Bennett looked about at a snowfield that lay unbroken, except for the giant pines, until it dropped off the edge of the height. The air was piercingly cold and sweet.

"They said it hadn't snowed much up here," he said, his tone bitter. "Damn if it hasn't had a blizzard already, it looks like."

The Yaqui turned from his pack, freshly bound to his horse. "Not much snow for this mountain," he said. "I see it higher than horse, many time, in place like this. Now it not over fetlock."

That was true. Shivering, Bennett moved upward again, hoping that he would never see this so-called pass deeper in snow than it was at this moment. His long journey through the desert country in August had thinned his blood, and the cold was striking into his bones.

They came to the top of the pass on the third day of climbing. On either hand the sharp-edged peaks clawed at the sky, their tops hidden in cloud that held, Cleve was sure, more snow than mist. The pass itself was a wrinkle between the adjacent mountains, and the river that had made it was at this place only a brook.

Could his people get here in time to make it over the pass before things became too difficult for horse and man alike? He hoped so, for many reasons.

Cucha seemed to be wondering, too. When they looked down the other side of the pass, its windings hidden by folds of snow-clad rock and stands of thick-trunked pines, the Yaqui nodded decisively.

"We get hell out," he said. "Go back quick, tell Walters. They better come soon. This place very dangerous when snowstorm come."

"How long, you think, till it's impassable?" Cleve asked, looking up warily at the frosted heights that seemed to hang over his head, their tops hidden in what seemed to be a light mist, but might well be snow at that higher elevation.

"Maybe so two hand of days. Maybe so not," the Yaqui replied.

Without another word they turned, this time to the easier and faster side of the river, now a trickle emerging from icicle-studded rock, and headed down again. Cleve had a hard time holding back, for his instinct was to plunge headlong down the mountain and gallop at full speed to guide the party onward.

But he controlled himself. He was, after all, a Cheyenne by adoption, and they never allowed impulse to override good sense. Second Son, traveling with the party below, would be ashamed if he lost his discipline at this point in their journey.

chapter

—22—

The riders in the Walters party had passed the stone-topped hill and crossed much of the terrible country along the foot of the range, finding their journey helped considerably by the markers left by the two scouts.

Yet with every mile Second Son knew more surely that something was going wrong. At last she asked the Ute woman to ride near her. She would never have believed that the big woman would become the comfort of her journey, but it was turning out to be true. Often she felt the anxious gaze of Two Big Feet as she turned in her saddle to check on her.

But the Cheyenne kept her face still, her back straight. The robe she wore hid her thickening body from those around her, and she wanted only that single one of her fellow travelers to suspect that she was in trouble.

Even Walters, when he asked how she fared, was answered with a noncommittal grunt. She suspected that Cleve had asked him to watch her, and she, as a warrior, resented the implication that she needed such care.

They came to the river near noon, five days after Cleve had left the company, finding it fairly well filled. When she asked Quiet Coyote why it should have so much water at this time of year, he pointed upward.

"It snow up there," he said. "When sun shine, snow melt. Run away down river to this place. Soon will not melt. Then will be too late to cross pass. We hurry."

She agreed with that advice, and Walters, too, seemed to take it to heart. The riders moved as quickly as possible along the nearer bank of the stream, following a very clear rock sign left by the Yaqui. She could see that he and Cleve had crossed to the other side of the stream, but they indicated that those following should take this route. It became evident that they had taken the other way for a particular reason.

At last Second Son suggested that the scouts must have gone along the farther bank of the river in order to check this one out from that direction. It made sense, too.

As she led Shadow up the steep track, slippery with horse dung and loose gravel, Second Son kept an eye on the ledge beyond the deepening chasm. She could see the spots where shale had slipped or rock had split as the climbers moved upward; those two could easily have checked the condition of this track in the same manner.

If there had been a dangerous place, she knew that Cleve or Cucha would have set some signal of warning on their edge of the ravine. Plodding heavily upward, she wondered where the scouts might be now. She was beginning to long for Cleve's strong arm, for her body threatened to betray her, now that this bad pregnancy was becoming a real problem.

Two Big Feet, riding just ahead of her, dropped back in a wider space. "You need to rest," she told Second Son. "You look bad in face. Not want to have big trouble before we get over pass."

That was true, and when a runnel descending beside a great pine tree offered a place to pull out of the line, she led Shadow into its cut. The horses thumped past, led by men and women too weary to notice someone resting there.

When the last had passed, Second Son tugged her mare back into the path again. After her short pause, she felt that she could get her breath again, and the nagging pain between her hips had eased somewhat.

The last of the packhorses was now well ahead of her, observed by the tail man responsible for watching for strays or problems among the animals. Toosh was the one taking that position now, and he occasionally looked back at her.

As she pushed her heavy feet up and over rough spots and rocks, she felt that she was falling behind, but she found that she could not manage to hurry now. When he called back to ask if she needed help, however, she could not bring herself to ask for it. She was trapped between her warrior pride and her female problem.

The cliff at her right seemed to sway. The path wriggled like a snake before her feet, making her feel dizzy and sick. Still, she climbed as best she could after the retreating party of travelers, clinging with damp fingers to Shadow's rein and wishing that she had asked Two Big Feet to wait with her while she rested.

The wind that rushed down the narrow cut was cold now, colder than before. Snow began to patch the rocks and the pines she passed, and from time to time pellets of sleet stung her forehead or her cheek. A snowstorm was sweeping down the mountain toward the travelers, she knew, but she could do nothing but keep moving as long as possible.

At last Second Son realized that she could no longer see the rider ahead, no longer hear hooves ringing on stones or the voices of her companions. She was alone on the side of this terrible mountain, and it was time for something drastic to happen inside her.

The unease of the past months was coming to a climax. She knew that she was about to lose this child, here amid the growing storm; with the wind wailing down the cut and over the rocks, there was no way to make anyone hear if she called. Even the Ute was gone into the swirling mixture of snow and sleet.

Now Second Son clung to the cliff edging the track, feeling her way along with numbing fingers. Behind her, Shadow snorted and nudged her back with her nose, wanting to get out of the blast.

Second Son understood her need. As a knife of pain thrust up through her body, she bent almost double, breathing carefully and trying to ease the cramp. When she could straighten again, she knew that she must find shelter or die here with only her mare for company.

It was a good day to die—all days were that—but this was not how she would have chosen to go, killed by her own baby. She would have chosen to die with her lance or her bow in hand, facing an honorable enemy.

Second Son leaned against the stone beside her for a long moment, and a picture she had held in her mind for most of her adult life appeared behind her eyes. . . .

The sun blazed above the plain, marking the distorted shape of her body and her horse on the dun-colored grass. The lance in her hand fluttered with feathers, and those in her braid whispered softly in the breeze as she prepared to attack.

She kicked Shadow in the ribs and raised the lance toward the sun. "Eeeeeeyiiiiiii!" she cried as the horse plunged toward the waiting warrior, now urging his own mount toward their confrontation.

She felt his lance stab deep into her vitals. . . .

She woke to the reality that this was not that enemy. At that moment, her seeking hand found a break in the cliff wall. She felt about, finding that this was no crack but a considerable gap leading into a niche in the cliff. As the wind swirled the snow aside for a moment, she could see that a cluster of young pines had taken root there and grown into a thicket.

She tugged Shadow into the break, out of the worst of the wind. It was again thick with snow, and the clouds had darkened the day to almost night. She felt her way into the thicket, where Shadow pushed past her toward the farther edge, where a bit of grass had managed to grow. There the wind did not reach except as a swirl of cold air.

Second Son, warrior of the Burning Hearts, pulled her bedroll off the back of the mare and dropped it into the shelter of the fragrant pines. The ground was a mix of snow and pine straw; there she spread her buffalo hide and knelt on it, pulling it about her shoulders and over her head.

In that tiny tipi, her body's warmth was held close to her, and she breathed a sigh of relief. Then her entire attention was occupied with a series of racking cramps.

She lay carefully on her side, knees drawn up as the muscles inside her worked to expel the infant. Time disappeared from her consciousness as she labored to free herself of this unhealthy pregnancy.

Even survival was no longer a consideration. She must do what must be done, and then she would deal with what came after. If she died here, that was the way of life. Either way, this must come to an end.

Warm blood gushed from her body, and compelling contractions moved her to their rhythms. She made no sound, though she felt gasps tearing at her throat.

Something touched her bowed back questioningly, pulling her out of that concentration. "Shadow?" she moaned.

Again the touch came, and hands pulled the robe from her face. "I come back," said Two Big Feet. "You no follow. I know what happen."

With a sigh of relief, Second Son saw the small fire the woman had kindled against the far wall of rock that confined the thicket's small cup. A pot of snow was already melting there, and the woman turned from her patient to take from her medicine bag a handful of big dark seeds.

But Second Son had no time or strength for watching. All the energy she had was directed toward relieving her stressed body. Again she lost track of time's passing, and only when the Ute lifted her head and put a horn cup to her lips did she understand that the woman had prepared some medicinal dose.

"Cottonseed from trade tribe. Make everything come out. Drink now." The rim of the cup clicked on her clenched teeth; using the power of her will, Second Son relaxed her jaw and swallowed the nasty dose.

After what seemed a very long time, there came a dreadful rush of spasms as the fetus was expelled. Two Big Feet was busy for a long time after that, but Second Son lay spent, eyes closed, feeling a sense of loss and depression that she had not expected.

She dropped into a sleep that seemed to drag her deep into darkness. Only when the Ute pulled her up and slapped her did she wake fully.

"Must go," the woman said. "If not now, we freeze on mountain. Must catch up with riders. You hear?"

Second Son knew she was correct. They might well add their bones to the tally of this pass, if they did not move at once.

She sighed raggedly, settled the moss packing the Ute had used to control her bleeding, and rose to her feet. Somehow she must get herself onto Shadow's back and catch up with the rest of the party, if she was to survive at all.

Though she felt like a broken twig, Second Son's muscles answered her demands, and she managed to mount Shadow. Then Two Big Feet led the horses and the exhausted rider back out into the terrible weather beyond the opening.

Grateful for the woman's care, Second Son realized that her huge friend's stature might well make the difference between survival and death. A person as tall as Cleve could make a way through drifts that one of her own height simply could not manage.

Already the Ute had pulled her robe over her head as she walked ahead, feeling out a way for the following horses. Second Son felt her own blood freezing on the buffalo robe, but she was glad of its weight about her as she was carried along on Shadow's familiar back.

She wondered where Cleve might be . . . had he perished in this storm? But that was too difficult to believe. In a haze of snow and cold and exhaustion, she rode blindly to meet whatever might come.

chapter

— 23 —

There had been no danger going up the mountain, except for the ever-present perils of the trail. Cleve had not expected anything to hinder the trip down again, as he and Cucha led their beasts along the much wider and more passable ledge on the other side of the river. They pushed a bit harder than was quite wise, in fact.

The pass behind them was already wrapped in cloud, and snow was beginning to whirl about his back. The wind at the back of his neck was colder than it had been only hours before. He understood too well that unless the Walters party hurried its pace, the entire group might well be snowed in along this narrow defile, where they would starve to death if a thaw did not come quickly. And at this time of year that was virtually impossible.

The Yaqui, ahead of him, seemed to be thinking the same, for he also was traveling at a pace that seemed rash. Yet on this wider track there should have been no major threat. The edge shelved back rather than slanting out over the stream, making the trek less intimidating than their upward journey.

Occasional breaks in the wall of the river canyon offered secure places to rest the horses, and there were even bushes or pine and aspen trees, as well as a bit of tan grass, in some of them. No matter what their hurry, the horses must rest, and those nooks offered a good place for that, out of the wind.

The pauses to rest shortened as the day waned and the icy wind began whipping about their ears, as if to slice them from their heads. Yet they had to stop from time to time. In the late afternoon Cleve was ready for a rest when they pulled their mounts into a shelter.

It was almost dark now, and he knew that even at top speed it would take most of another day to get to the foot of the mountain. There was no other good place to camp for a very long way, and falling off the mountain would help nobody.

"Maybe we'd better build us a fire and camp here," he said to the Yaqui.

Cucha nodded and began gathering deadfall beneath the four big pines whose needled branches roofed the small space. Cleve scraped bare a patch of rock in the middle of the space and laid the fire Indian fashion, peaked into a pyramid.

Once the fire was kindled, the warmth was trapped by the stony walls and the pines, and the two men began to thaw. They chewed jerky and drank coffee boiled in the small pot Cleve had in his pack, more for the internal heat than anything else. It almost thawed his blood enough to circulate again, Cleve found.

As they squatted by the fire, their robes draped about their shoulders, there came a sound from the back of the rocky niche. A stone rolled from some unseen height, sending the horses plunging and snorting; then a roar brought Cleve upright, reaching for his flintlock, which he had primed and set ready to hand, in this unknown place.

This disturbance was caused by a bear, and it was best to shoot him with his Hawken. Arrows sometimes only irritated the big beasts, and no one wanted to share his camp with an irritated bear.

Cleve retreated behind a pine bole at one side while Cucha moved the other way. The blaze in the middle of the space flickered over the rocks and lighted to dreadful clarity the shape of a huge animal ambling down the steep runnel that led up to their camping place.

Cleve checked the priming pan, aimed, and let fly. The blast of the weapon, followed by a pall of black smoke, was shocking. One of the horses screamed, and the clatter of hooves on rock told him that it had fled into the cold night beyond the cut.

He whistled once, in case it was Socks, but there was an answering whinny near at hand. Yet there was no time to worry about the horse . . . a bear could kill two men without realizing it had exerted itself, and he didn't intend for that to happen.

Cleve moved cautiously out of his hiding place, his hands busy with ramrod, powder, ball, and wadding. Beyond the fire, he could see a tangle of struggling shadows. Cucha was now engaged, hand-to-hand, with the bear. The resulting grunts and gasps might be those of either of the combatants. Both were gruff enough for either.

As he passed the fire Cleve kicked fresh fuel onto the coals. Then he sidled around the intervening tree trunks to see how he might help his companion.

The replenished blaze brightened, and he saw Cucha hugged tightly in the grasp of the biggest bear he had seen in years. Cleve paused to think. If he shot, he would most likely hit the Yaqui, so he laid aside his flintlock and took out his knife.

It was time to see if he could kill a bear with a steel blade. Years ago he'd done it with an ax; by contrast that looked much easier than his present task. An ax had a much longer handle, for one thing.

It was best to work his way around the pair, approaching the bear from behind, for he had never had any ambition to go face-to-face with one of the big creatures. The two were still stamping around the small clearing, now moving toward the fire.

Indeed, even as Cleve tried to position himself to attack, the bear backed into the fire and upset the coffeepot. Scalded and scorched simultaneously, the beast roared with pain and fright.

He leaned backward, pawing at the air and letting the Yaqui drop to the ground at his feet. Then he danced about the clearing, roaring, before going to all fours to find his quarry again.

Cleve sighed. Then he moved forward, despite the urgent pleadings of his sense of self-preservation, and rammed into the bear side on, driving the knife to its hilt in the thick-furred hide behind the shoulder. That didn't slow the animal, which wheeled through the campfire with frightening speed to face him.

The knife was carried out of his grasp, still embedded in its hide. Cleve was now weaponless as the bear began rising again to its full height, some two feet above Cleve's considerable stature.

A stick, one end a glowing mass of coals from the fire, rolled under Cleve's foot. Without taking his gaze from the bear, he bent to take it up. Then he whirled it above his head and ran directly at the animal, shouting at the top of his lungs. Something raw and hot and crazy took over his body and his mind as he attacked the creature, and he couldn't have stopped if he'd tried.

The echoes from the surrounding cliffs were deafening. The bear, now feeling its wound, stunned by the noise, frightened by the wild figure and the blazing pine branch stabbing at its dazzled eyes, gave a despairing roar and fled back up the runnel down which it had come, leaving behind the stink of scorched fur.

His chest heaving with a combination of breathlessness, madness, and terror, Cleve dropped the stick back onto the fire and turned to the unconscious Indian. Cucha was breathing, but his back was tracked with parallel claw marks that went deep.

He was pale, for an Indian, ashen almost, and that worried Cleve, too. Had the bear squeezed something inside him hard enough to kill him?

But it was best to treat such raw wounds while their owner was out of it. Cleve moved behind the biggest pine and pulled out the pack he had dropped there, out of the way.

Second Son insisted that he carry an assortment of her healing herb mixtures and a chunk of tallow. That came in handy for anything from waterproofing moccasins to sealing wounds, and he was thankful that he had it now.

Once he had put medicine on the long cuts, he'd melt the tallow and smear it over all, holding in the ointment and the blood as well. He hoped.

The small bag that contained a mix of white pine pitch and plantain root was tucked into the corner of his pack, and he set it beside the fire to warm while he cleaned Cucha's back. Blood enough to stock an entire tribe of Yaqui seemed to have leaked out of the man, so Cleve gathered handfuls of snow and scrubbed it onto the raw flesh until the bleeding slowed and stopped.

Now the Yaqui's back was almost blue with cold, but the warmed pitch adhered to it well, filling the cuts and bringing the skin color back to something more nearly normal. By the time Cleve was finishing that, Cucha began to flinch at his touch, though no groan left the man's lips. Even in a state of unconsciousness, it was clear that complaining was not a trait of his kind.

The hot tallow was another matter. Cucha heaved upward with a yell, both hands pushing against the ground, when it dribbled across the wounds. At once he calmed, understanding quickly that Cleve was helping him. He lay flat again, letting the painful process go forward.

When Cleve was done, he put away his supplies, speaking quietly to his patient. "You had me worried there, Cucha. I thought that bear had got you for certain. But you're a tough old bastard. I think you're just going to have an interesting new set of scars to show off to the womenfolks when everything heals up again."

"Bear?" asked the Yaqui, his cheek against the pine straw that the fire had dried. "You kill him?"

"Not me!" Cleve protested. "You're the one who thought you could beat that critter bare-handed. I got him a good one, but it cost me my best knife. He carried it away with him, stuck in his side."

He tried to chuckle, though he still felt shaken and weak-kneed. "Even that didn't faze him, though. He didn't take off until I tried to ram a burning stick right up his nose. That scared him.

"Of course, it helped that he burned his feet when he backed into the fire. He spilt all the coffee, or I'd get you to drink a cup."

He bent over Cucha. "You feel like sitting up? I want to see if those edges will hold when you move. I have a gut feeling that we ought to get out of here, because that bear just might forget how scared he was and come back to finish up the job he started. This time I might be the one he wants to hug, and I don't like the idea one little bit."

Again Cucha pushed himself up, and this time he made no sound, although his breathing was ragged and unsteady. Cleve didn't try to help. With the problems the Yaqui had, any touch was going to hurt like hell. Best to let him see how far he could make it. Then, if he needed help, he had sense enough to ask for it.

When Cucha was sitting in his normal cross-legged position, Cleve could see that one shoulder was higher than the other, as if it might be dislocated. He shuddered. Once he'd had a dislocated shoulder, back on the farm as a boy. He still remembered how it hurt.

But there was no way to adjust this one as his father had done, by shifting the affected arm with one hand while bracing the other hand against his back. That back didn't need any more stress, and pressure might make the bleeding start again.

"How's it feel inside?" he asked. "I was afraid he might have busted your ribs or something. You looked mighty bad. Fact is, you still don't look any too wonderful."

Cucha straightened his back slowly, the control showing in his lack of expression as he managed it. He moved his left hand, which responded normally. He flexed the fingers of his right, and then even the stalwart warrior winced.

"All right inside, I think," he said. "Not good in shoulder. But we go. Bear come back, maybe so. Not want to be here when that happen."

"The other horse ran off," Cleve said, rising. "Socks is over there against the cliff, watching out for any more bears. You can go on him. I couldn't ride anyway, out there in the snow and the dark. I'll lead him, and maybe down a way we'll find your animal. Both packs can go behind you. Here, let me help you up."

He whistled Socks over, saddled him, and gave Cucha a boost as the Indian's strong legs carried him onto the animal's back. Wrapping the wounded man in a double layer of robes, Cleve tied on the packs, one behind, one on Socks's right side, away from the cliff as they descended. There was no sense in risking having the pack push the horse too close to the edge.

He left the fire burning. Here, amid the snowy stones of the niche, it could do no harm, and it might keep the bear from coming down to sniff about their abandoned camp, possibly to follow them down the canyon.

The fire's comfortable flicker cast giant shadows against the walls of the gap as he led Socks and his burden out into the terrible night. He felt somehow saddened when its glow was left behind and there was only the wail of the wind and the terrible slash of snow at his back.

chapter
— 24 —

The string of riders had struggled upward into the wind until the light failed. Malachi had led his horse so long that he felt as if his fingers were frozen around the reins, and Beeville, just ahead, was slogging along through the deepening snow with feet that had to be half-frozen.

It was time to halt the column for the night. Traveling along this narrow, dizzy cliffside in the dark was work for fools, and Walters had never considered himself to be one. Yet you couldn't stop in this wind-blasted canyon with your people strung all up and down the narrow ledge. If they didn't freeze where they huddled, the horses would go over the edge—or people would.

There came a shout from up ahead. Quiet Coyote appeared through the thickening snow. When he came even with the Ute, Walters paused and asked, "Is there a place to camp somewhere up there?"

The Ute put his face near his and shouted, "Follow. I take you there soon. Good place, wide enough. Come fast. Wind rise, snow come worse."

Feeling a surge of hope, Walters passed the word to Douglas, who was just behind him. "Pass it down the line," he yelled, and the man turned to obey his order. Every one of his people was going to take heart when they heard the news.

Beeville had waited up ahead beside the Pawnee, but when Quiet Coyote slid past them again, they picked up their feet with renewed energy. The prospect of a fire, shelter from the wind, and something hot to eat was one to rouse all to new efforts.

The sky turned dark as clouds settled closer about the mountain. Only the paleness of the snow gave any visibility at all, and that was fitful, for the wind blew it into eyes and down necks. Inured as he was to such brutal journeys, Malachi found himself shivering. Maybe Prévot wasn't the only one getting too old for such goings-on.

At last the Ute shouted again, his voice carried away down the canyon on the merciless wind. "Turn here!"

Beeville and the Pawnee disappeared. Then Walters found himself leading his mount around an elbow of stone, into a high meadow enclosed by towering cliffs on three sides. Abutments of rock leaned toward each other, partially closing the entrance to this unexpected paradise, in which clumps of alder were interrupted by towering pines, whose needles whistled shrilly in the wind above the sheltering walls.

The floor of the enclosure was relatively free of snow, because of the growth and also because this blizzard was traveling sideways more than drifting straight down. Before he could pull his pack off his horse, the Indian women were gathering deadfall into two big pyramids, one on either side of the meadow.

By the time the rest of the column straggled into shelter, those fires were roaring comfortably and the pots were already filled with snow, ready for cooking to begin. Even before the warmth began to spread, the red-gold light filled Walters with relief.

Malachi was as exhausted as the next man, but the habit of a lifetime held, and he counted as his party came into sight. The tally went on and on as groups of two and three continued to appear, but at last there seemed to be no more. Even the extra horses had been driven into the little valley, to shelter against the wall with the others.

He looked about, checking off names in his notebook. Then he went over the count again.

When he turned to Douglas, he felt as if someone had hit him in the belly. "Bennett's wife isn't here. Neither is Two Big Feet. How in hell did that happen? Their packhorses are over there with the bunch in the corner, but I don't see either one of their mounts."

He found Toosh Marlow, who had been the last one in charge at the rear of the herd. "You see Bennett's wife or the Ute woman back along the trail?" he asked the man.

Toosh looked up from his bedroll. "Second Son was right behind me, I think. She looked like she was havin' trouble, but when I asked her if she needed help, she said to go on ahead. She'd catch up later.

"Come to think of it, the Ute woman come back down the trail after a while and passed me. I figgered she was goin' to see about Second Son. Never thought another thing about it, though."

Which was just like Toosh. He was a good man if you made him understand exactly what he had to do, but he wasn't one for thinking on his own.

"Oh, God!" Walters groaned. "Those two women're someplace down there in all this snow. Cleve asked me to take care of his woman—she's carryin', and he thought she was havin' problems. Dammit to hell!"

He stepped to the drafty gap leading onto the track and stared out into the blinding swirls of snow. He'd have to saddle one of the spare horses and go back down. Bennett had undertaken a dangerous job for him, and he couldn't do any less than keep his promise.

Even as he turned to find a fresher mount, there came the clatter of hooves higher up the track. A desperate horse dashed past him into the shelter of the stony walls and the comfort of other horses and the fires of men.

Malachi hurried after him and caught up as the animal halted among the nickering bunch in the corner of the meadow.

"This Cucha's mount," Quiet Coyote said at his shoulder. "Very frighten, this horse. Maybe so he throw Cucha off trail, back there?" He sounded dubious, for throwing the Yaqui was an exercise that many horses had tried; none any of the company knew about had succeeded.

"We can't know for sure," Walters said, running his hands down the animal's legs, checking its hide for injuries.

"I can't find any wound, that's for sure. Maybe they stopped to camp and something spooked him, you think?"

Coyote stared at the horse. Then he gazed past the intervening trees and the busy people toward the opening to the canyon. The Indian nodded. "Hear nothing but wind. Nobody chase him, I think." The Ute looked as concerned as his enigmatic face could manage.

"Well, however it is, I've got to push my weary bones out into *that* and look for those damn women. Might as well walk, because a horse is nothin' but a liability out there. You comin'?" he asked.

Coyote turned that dark gaze on him, and he saw impatience in the black eyes. "One is my woman," he said. "We go now?"

Walters nodded. All too soon the brief respite in the warmth and light was behind him as he trudged down the crazy track, with the wind trying to push him onto his face. Behind him came Coyote, and only an occasional touch at his shoulder told him the Ute was there, for the storm now howled like a puma, blanking out any other sound.

The traces of the party's passing were already almost obliterated, and the fluttering flame of the torches the two carried only blinded them. Very soon they doused them in a snowdrift and continued by touch against the cliff.

Walters understood that sort of travel all too well, for already on this journey he had lost several of his people and more horses through falls into canyons much like this one. He was going to stick like glue to that stony wall at his left.

The way seemed endless, and even wrapped in furs as he was, he was chilled through by the time he bumped headlong into a bulky object blocking the track. He gasped with shock, and before he could reach to feel what it might be, other hands came out to touch his fur-capped head, his face.

Then he knew; only Two Big Feet would be walking here. And if she were here, then Second Son would be behind her.

Coyote came up beside him and grunted into his ear.

"Found 'em!" Walters yelled, and a horse squealed in reply. He felt his way past the Ute woman, found the side of a horse, and reached up to touch a chilly burden on its back.

"Second Son?" he screamed, but the wind carried his cry away down the valley.

A cold hand touched his face. A finger tapped three times, reassuringly, and he sighed with relief. If he had been forced to meet Cleve Bennett with the news that his wife had been lost in the storm, he would never have lived down the shame.

They turned into the wind again, and its sharp edges of sleet, its almost solid blast of snow tried to batter them back down the mountain. It was going to take a long time to get back to camp, Walters knew, and he wondered how the woman on the horse was faring.

If Second Son had not had problems, she would be walking with Two Big Feet. He hoped devoutly that she would not freeze to death up there before they could find shelter again.

If the walk down the trail had been terrible, the trip back up was too painful to think about. Only the need to set one foot before the other, time after time, to make frozen muscles continue their work, and the thought of a waiting fire and hot food kept Malachi going.

It was almost impossible to move into that wind now. The icy blast seemed intent upon pushing them all back down the track and over the edge of the canyon. Only when they turned a dogleg bend was there shelter, and there Walters paused in the relative quiet.

"How you makin' it?" he asked.

"I am here," Second Son murmured. "I am alive. Don't worry about me, Mr. Walters, for I will stick on this horse until I freeze or get to camp." Her voice was incredibly calm for someone in her predicament, and he wondered once more at her stoicism.

But it was time to move again, and he followed behind the Ute woman's horse, glad of the shelter its body gave. When at last they turned into the fire-bright mountain meadow, he felt as if everything about him except his slogging heart had congealed into ice.

He handed the reins of the horse to Douglas, who led it toward the fire. Malachi shrugged off his thick mantle of snow and buffalo hide and gave a deep shiver.

"I've never b-been so c-cold in my life," he said to Quiet Coyote. "Lead me to the fire, Coyote. I don't think I can move."

A smile almost appeared on the Ute's face. He, too, was shivering, his face bluish with chill, but he reached a dark hand to help Walters along, and together they came to the nearest of the fires. The steam from the pot bubbling there smelled like heaven, and Malachi dropped to sit beside the fire and wait for someone to fill his tin mug with stew.

He had the mug almost to his lips—he could nearly taste the food, relish it as it went down his gullet—when another disturbance distracted him. He turned, ready to blast the person who interrupted. . . .

The way down the mountain was purest hell. Cleve began to wonder if they'd make it without staggering blindly off the invisible edge of the ledge. Even as he struggled along, held up at times by his grip on Socks's cheek strap, he thought more than once how easy it would be just to lie down and drift into that snow-sleep that was perhaps the easiest way of all to die.

After a long time, during which he grew colder and more exhausted as he moved along, he found himself down on his knees, already slumping forward onto the snow. But the young stallion nosed his neck and nickered in his ear, bringing him back to consciousness. He pulled himself up by the animal's mane and moved back along his snowy side to check on the Yaqui.

Cucha was a bundle of snow-covered robes, invisible against the stony cliff behind him. Cleve touched the bundle, shook what he determined to be a knee to wake the Indian.

Cucha didn't move for a long moment, and Cleve found himself wondering if the injured man had died of the cold, sitting there on top of Socks, frozen to the saddle. Again he shook that knee while the wind whooped down the canyon and tried to shove him off the trail.

After a heart-chilling wait, he felt the knobby knee under his hand move, just a bit. Then a hand emerged from the stiff robes and tapped his shoulder. Cleve felt a surge of relief, for though he had never been particularly close to Cucha, he found that their shared perils on this mission had welded their lives together in some indefinable way. Knowing his charge was still alive gave him fresh strength as he turned again to feel his way down the track.

His feet were numb, and his fingers, even wrapped in deerhide, felt as if they were about to drop off. He found that it was very hard to keep his mind focused on his purpose, for he tended to drift into strange dreams.

Working his careful way around an icy abutment onto another angle of the trail, he came face-to-face with his old enemy vision. That bull buffalo, snorting steam, coat glinting with frost, eyes gleaming red, stood there, tossing his horns, daring him to try to pass.

Cleve's heart drummed, and he found himself suddenly terribly alert, aware that he was being misled by the cold and the noise of the wind. No buffalo stood there. Only another dim stretch of trail . . . but at its end there seemed to be the warm glow of light.

Had he found Walters and the rest of the party, camped in one of the small meadows that studded the mountain? The thought lent his wavering legs new strength, and he tugged on Socks's reins, pulling the horse forward more quickly.

When he drew near enough to see the flicker of light on the leaning stones forming the entrance into the small meadow, Cleve straightened his back and stepped forward into the shelter of the high walls that circled that spot. Trees rose there, hiding the merciless storm above. People moved among them, and horses nickered a greeting to Socks.

Cleve tugged again on the reins and staggered toward the nearest of the fires. A well-wrapped shape came to meet him, and he recognized Walters. The grin he felt growing across his face seemed to crack his almost frozen skin, but he let it rip. He'd made it, by God!

Walters watched Cleve Bennett lead Socks, on whose back the Yaqui slumped. As they drew near, Bennett raised a pair of bloodshot eyes and recognized the leader of the party.

"Mal'chi," he said, through chattering teeth. "Thought maybe we'd never get h-here. S-second Son all right?"

Malachi felt a wave of thankfulness that he had taken that terrible journey down the canyon. He could honestly say, "She's here. I think she may've lost the baby, though. Once you warm up, you'd better go check on her, Cleve."

He felt proud that he was able to say all that without his own teeth chattering. When he turned toward Freeman Douglas, he found the man at his side, wrapping a warm robe around Bennett while the Yaqui's woman did the same for her man.

"Cucha's m-mighty bad hurt," Cleve said over his shoulder as he followed Malachi's pointing hand toward his wife. "B-better get the best he-healers ahold of him. He's some m-man."

Then Bennett was gone. Walters settled once more to his warm stew, feeling that his entire group had earned a night of rest, whatever perils tomorrow might bring.

chapter 25

By the time he found the bedroll where Second Son lay, bloodless and exhausted, Cleve was almost ready to pass out himself. But he lay beside her, touched her face, and saw her eyes open.

"Yellow Hair," she murmured. "You have come at last." She reached to touch his cheek, but her hand dropped quickly to lie on her blanket. It was plain that she had been wearied almost past endurance.

He saw movement from the corner of his eye, and he looked up to see Two Big Feet standing over them, looking like a tree herself. She held a horn cup, which she offered to him as he sat up.

The stew was delicious, rich and hot. His belly, which had felt as if it were glued to his backbone, began to fill; he felt new energy run through his veins. He watched, still eating slowly and carefully, while the Ute examined his wife, repacking moss to control her bleeding.

It was amazing to Cleve that such a big, tough woman could be so gentle, so deft as she did her work. She sat beside Second Son, waiting, obviously, to talk with him when he finished his food. He drained the last of the broth and sighed.

"You saved my life," he said to the Ute. "And I think you may've saved Second Son, too. How is she?"

"Good now," said the woman. "Have hard head, though. Wait behind when pain start. I go back to see. Good thing. She no have more baby, maybe so. I see such thing before."

Cleve felt a moment of sadness. He had begun to look forward with pleasure to having another baby to play with and teach, another child to show how to live in this world where self-reliance was the key to survival. The thought that they might have no more was not one he liked, but he still had his wife. Together, they made a helluva pair, able to deal with just about anything.

But Two Big Feet was not done. "Give hand," she ordered him.

He held out his right hand, which was frosty looking still. She rubbed it with snow. Then she soaked it in water warmed at the fire until pain shot through his entire hand and up his arm. Frostbite was always a problem, but this big Ute seemed to know what she was doing.

When she was done, he thought to ask about Cucha. "He will live," she told him, taking the horn cup and rising. "You, too. Now sleep. I think we not move until after storm."

When he opened his eyes again, Cleve could see that the sky was lighter above the overhanging branches of the pines, though snow still whipped across it and continued to accumulate on the treetops. His bones felt as if he'd been beaten with sticks, and he groaned as he pulled himself up to sit beside his sleeping wife.

Others were still dozing, though most of the women and a few of the men were already busy mending gear and clothing or tending the fires. With the protection of cliffs and trees in this meadow, the air here was much warmer than it was out in the canyon, he knew. It would be madness to leave a sheltered spot with fuel at hand to tackle the climb again. Only when the blizzard died would that be feasible.

He rose and shook himself before wandering to a nearby snowbank to wash his face with snow. Once he felt fairly human again, he looked about for Walters, who was, he found, sitting beside the Yaqui under a clump of alders. Cucha looked perfectly normal, as if his encounter with the bear had never happened.

When he joined the two, Cleve saw that beneath his robe the Yaqui's body was wrapped with soft deerhide, bound 'round and 'round to hold those claw marks on his back together. He dropped to sit on the pine straw beside him.

"How you feeling, Cucha? Looks as if they fixed you up fine."

Walters, who had looked pretty frozen last night, as Cleve recalled, grinned. "The women were considerable impressed with your doctorin'," he said. "The blood had clotted, and the wounds were stuck nice and tight with whatever it was you put on 'em. Whatever that was, I'd like to know your recipe."

Cucha grunted. "Next time you fight bear," he said. "Not good thing to do. That bear quick or I get away before he grab me."

But Walters was more interested in hearing a report on their mission. "How'd you find it up there?" he asked.

Cleve poked a twig into the pine needles, thinking back on the terrible night. "It was pretty well covered before that last storm ran us down the mountain," he said. "Not too deep to travel, but another couple like this one and it will be. You intend to try traveling before the storm lets up?"

Walters shook his head. "If I hadn't had to go back out in it to bring in your wife and Two Big Feet, I might've been dumb enough to try it. Now I know it's just a fancy way to die. We'll wait here until it eases off. Then we'll try it again." He looked sharply at Cleve.

"You see anything really bad up ahead?" he asked. "I watched the other side, and it looked undercut in lots of places. I'd hate to have the ledge cave in with a bunch of my folks on it."

Cleve looked at Cucha. "I watch," the Yaqui said to Walters. "Tell Yellow Hair to watch feet. I keep eye on this side. Not bad place like that, just narrow, slick. Put man here, man here, man here. . . ." He dotted in widely spaced twig marks.

Cleve bent forward to see. Then he nodded. "Keep too

much weight off any one spot. Space 'em out so that if one bunch slips, it won't take another down with 'em. It'll take longer to get the whole party across, but we stand a lot better chance of making it with most of us alive.

"That's no play game, out there," he went on. "If the trail doesn't get you, the cold will, and I can swear to that. I almost went off myself, dreaming things that weren't there at all." He thought again of that old buffalo, wondering if it had been a warning of things to come or a signal that Second Son was in danger behind the party.

It was agreed among the scouts that to move forward would be courting death. Beeville, always silent, always listening, nodded when Walters confirmed the decision. Taking chances was the business of every person there, but stupid chances were another thing entirely.

The day passed slowly after Cleve had checked his mounts and his packhorses. He mended moccasins and tattered robes, and then he sat and watched Second Son sleep. He'd wondered about such deep and unbroken sleep for someone who usually slept with one eye open, and at last he asked Two Big Feet about it.

"I give her medicine," said the Ute. "Make sleep. She need it, when we go."

It sounded smart to Cleve. If she was rested right down to her toenails by the time they left this shelter, she'd be able to make the demanding trip to the top of the pass. After that, he hoped that things would be just a bit easier.

Night came early, for clouds still hung thickly about the mountain and the wind still whistled past the gap leading into the meadow. Worn out with waiting, Cleve tended to

Second Son, who woke hungry and slept again as soon as she had eaten. Then he stretched out beside her again and closed his eyes, lulled by the quiet voices of their companions spaced around the meadow.

Overhead the pines shrilled in the wind, and he knew that when that noise eased, it might well be time to travel again. He wanted to be rested, of course, but he was eager to cross that pass before things became too bad to allow that to happen.

He woke often during the night, listening to the tones of the wind's voice. Before dawn, he woke again, and this time there was only a sighing above where the pine tops thrust above the sheltering walls of stone. The storm was over, or almost.

When the first light touched the strip of sky above, Cleve rose and Second Son sat up, alert and rested. "It is time to go?" she asked.

"I think so," he said. "Today we can get almost up to that damn pass, if we keep moving and are lucky."

She stood and tentatively stretched. Her color was close to normal now, and she moved more easily than she had in some time. Together they loaded their horses and joined the others about the big fire while Malachi explained the order of march.

It was time to make their move, and Cleve hoped they would make it to the other side. They'd earned the right, by now.

chapter

— 26 —

Malachi Walters stared down from the ridge that seemed to be the top of the world. Below, through a gap in the lower peaks, he could spot what seemed to be forest, the treetops dark green and thick.

He welcomed the sight, hoping that it meant game and water and warmth. Even though ridges and rolls and tumbles of mountains interrupted its pattern, it would be relatively easy to reach the shelter of those waiting trees.

Behind him, the long file of people and horses came over the pass, even leaner and tougher now than they had been when they left Green River back in August. If they had been a week later, he was certain that he would have lost far more than the half-dozen horses and two men who had not made it through the canyon.

He thought of Toosh Marlow with some respect. He'd been a good hand with the horses, had Toosh, though no one could say he was very smart. Too bad—but he'd gone quick, when an avalanche let loose right above him, sweeping those horses, Toosh, and Jim Stringer off into the canyon in a cloud of snow and rock. Walters shuddered, remembering the grating roar behind the column, and the awful stream of white that had poured over the end of the horse herd and the two riders there.

At the point where they had fallen, the stream was so far below that you couldn't even see it. There was no way either could have survived the drop, and if they had, there wasn't any way to get somebody down there to look for them. At that point he couldn't even stop the column to check on them, for there was more than a good chance that another avalanche might let loose and take everybody with it.

Still, Walters was a leader who hated losing either men or horses, and he wondered if he might have done something to prevent that loss. He was thinking about that as he waited for his people to cross over onto the downslope. But, so far, this side of the pass was not so steep, the trail down following a saddle of land and seeming to flank the next peak.

Already, Bennett and Quiet Coyote had scouted ahead and found their best way around that mountain. Beyond, they said, the way was almost clear of snow, and the game trails leading down into that distant forest were many and well marked. There were trees, they said, eyes wide and astonished, that were bigger around than any house they'd ever seen. Trees like mountains, Cleve had insisted.

The scouts' account of the giant trees was something he tended to discount. It had been a long journey, and young men were sometimes overenthusiastic. A tree as thick through as a house . . . that was unlikely. He hoped they would find easy travel, plenty of water, and fresh meat, all of which his group was ready to enjoy.

He turned to watch the very last of his column, the extra horses, come into sight and begin descending the track into the saddle. He thought again of Toosh, stringy and unwashed, but always faithful, and he sighed.

Then he fell in behind the last rider and began the long journey toward that forest, which was now hidden by intervening ridges of land. The stony bluffs shone pale gold, beyond the edge of the snowfield below, and strips of greenery interrupted the landscape with the promise of life. Malachi could hardly wait to get off this goddamn mountain.

Remaining behind the extra horses, he kept a watchful eye on the parts of the column he could see winding around the next height. Beyond that obstruction, hours later, he found that they must walk again, leading the horses along knife-edged ridges, but the forest was visibly nearer. As he moved onward Walters realized that the trees at the edge of the green area were extremely large, though not quite so huge as Cleve had said.

When he followed the horse herd into the treed area, he understood what the scouts had meant. Downslope, he could see trees, their trunks soaring skyward, that he could hardly believe existed. Men and horses looked like ants as they negotiated the game track around the tremendous roots of the first of the giants.

Malachi rode, neck cricked back, looking upward into the tops of those great trees, and he felt, for the first time in his life, an awe in the face of such tremendous living things. He shivered as they rode down through the forest, hearing the voices of birds that were invisible in the branches so high above him.

The forest extended for a very long distance. They camped that night in the shelter of its canopy, and the animals whose voices punctuated the night were subtly different, he thought, from those he had heard beyond the Sierras.

But it was time to move forward toward their goal. In a few days of riding the group left that forest and moved down into a long valley, edged on both sides with low ranges, the farther one cloaked in cloud or fog.

To Malachi's amazement, the valley looked like tame countryside, the grassland studded with graceful clumps of oaks. No scrub or untidy brush interrupted its stretches, and he felt that some careful gardener had been at work here. The thought, of course, was nonsense, but he couldn't quite discard it.

He knew that such rich country must hold inhabitants, and he sent the scouts and the Bennetts out ahead of the riders, checking for any possible danger. When Second Son came trotting back toward him, quite obviously carrying news, he was not surprised.

She pulled up and turned Shadow to keep pace with him and Beeville, at the head of the column. "We have found people," she said. "We cannot understand their language, but they know Sign. You might be interested in meeting them. They are with Cleve and Quiet Coyote, beyond that little hill."

Nodding to Douglas to keep an eye on the train, Malachi heeled his mount and trotted after the Cheyenne. As they crossed the low hill he could see that a group of people were spread out under a clump of oaks, evidently gathering acorns for their winter store. Children, naked as the day they were born, despite the cool weather, hung behind their elders, eyes wide and frightened.

The handful of adults stood warily, eyeing the white men as if making up their minds whether to run or to stay. Feeling something strange about their manner, Malachi dismounted and moved to stand beside Cleve.

"What're they so scared of? " he asked.

"Ask Second Son," Bennett said. "She's talked to the women. The men won't say much, even in Sign. Seems to me they've had some dealings with the Mexicans there and are scared out of their wits."

The Cheyenne moved nearer and said, "The women say the Long Robes take their children. They come here from the Great Water and hunt down these people, dragging them back to the great lodge they have built on the coast. There they make them into slaves, who tend the big-horned beasts they bring from the south and the strange fruits they have planted. Those who have escaped are very much afraid of them and they wondered, when they saw us, if we were some of those who guard the Long Robes."

Walters rubbed his chin thoughtfully. He'd heard tales from occasional wanderers, as well as from Jed Smith, about the methods the Spaniards had used and the Mexicans probably still did. Made sense, he'd thought, but now he wondered. These folks seemed harmless enough. There was no way they could pose a threat to people with white men's weapons and defenses.

Second Son's eyes were bright with anger. "I do not like what I hear, Mr. Walters. Be careful when we reach the Water. These men do not consider those unlike them to be men at all, and that may also include you and Yellow Hair and all your kind."

That, too, was something to consider. Malachi had had dealings with some of the priests when he traveled to Mexico, and he'd noticed their contempt for those who did not share their faith. He wondered if they had converted these poor heathen before enslaving them. Not that it would help their feelings much, he was sure.

"Give them some presents, Cleve, out of my bag. I feel kind of sorry for 'em—they look like pretty decent sorts. Makes me wonder what kind of welcome we'll have from those Long Robes once we get over the coast mountains to that bay where they have their fort and their mission."

But there was still a long way to go, and he was intent upon getting his people across this valley and the next range of mountains, which stood with their heads veiled in cloud. He watched silently as his men passed out gifts of steel knives and bright beads, of blankets and iron pots.

The people seemed amazed that white men would make gifts of any kind, and that puzzled Walters. Most whites began their dealings with the redskins by gift giving.

He turned his mount again toward the distant column of riders. There was a lot to think about, but it lay ahead. Now he had to get his butt back at the head of the line, where it belonged. Beeville had something to tell him, he knew, for the quiet man had asked him to spread his bedroll next to his that night.

Walters felt a quiver of excitement. There had been speculation for years about Beeville. Was he actually on a mission for the government that nobody knew about? That was the rumor that had followed him all the time he was in the Rockies, and now it seemed to Malachi that he might be carrying some message to the Mexican governor in Monterey from the president himself. Everybody knew that Andrew Jackson looked beyond the present boundaries of his country, and it would be like him to send a secret emissary to make contact with the Mexicans in California.

But that was only speculation, and he had other things to think about. As they rode forward across the lovely valley he spotted herds of deer and elk, and he sent hunters to bag fresh meat. It never hurt, when you knew you were to arrive unexpectedly, to bring your own food supply.

Before the column reached the foothills of the next range, Quiet Coyote, Cucha, and the Bennetts caught up, their packhorses laden with freshly killed carcasses. That put new heart into the riders, and by the time Walters had Douglas choose a campsite, the people he led seemed very cheerful.

He, too, was beginning to feet optimistic. Though nobody ever knew it, he always felt the possibility of failure stalking at his heels, which was one reason why he took such pains with his plans for any expedition.

Accident, unexpected enemies, terrible weather . . . all those lay in wait for even the most prudent and provident leader. But now most of those matters lay in the past, and the relatively short distance that probably remained before his group reached the coast should hold far fewer perils.

As he sat beside the big cookfire, watching Beeville

make up his mind to speak at last, Walters was more relaxed, less wary, than he had been since starting this difficult enterprise. When his employer rose and came to drop beside him near the fire, Malachi realized that Beeville, too, had been worried about the outcome of this journey.

Feeling a surge of curiosity, Walters bent forward and stirred the fire, making a cloud of sparks sputter upward. "So, Ben, you're ready to tell me what this is all about, are you?" he said quietly, his voice pitched to travel no farther than his companion.

Beeville looked at him, his expression startled. "You knew all along?" he asked. His fingers twiddled with a stick, and he leaned even closer to Malachi. "I thought everything was secret all the way."

Malachi chuckled. "I don't know anything I haven't been figuring out for myself all along," he said. "It's pretty plain that you've worked for President Jackson in the past—at least rumor makes it seem that way. And if you decided to head off toward the Pacific, I was pretty certain that it wasn't *just* to find new trapping grounds. Beaver never was your main interest, I always thought."

Ben Beeville seemed to study Malachi's face in the firelight, and Walters felt strange. He'd been working with this man for a long time now. Why would Beeville be so hesitant to trust him?

"This is the most important mission I've ever had," he said. "And a lot of what I know mustn't ever get out to anyone." He glanced about, but all the scouts, the mountain men, the women were busy sharing out the roasted meat in their individual camping spots. Not a soul was within earshot, except for two horses, which were dozing on their feet.

"Well, if you don't trust me now, you picked the wrong hombre to lead your party," Walters said. He poked the fire again to hide his irritation. "So spit it out or let it go, one or the other."

"I have official documents from our President to the *gobernador* in Monterey. These should, if the Mexican officials agree, open up travel and trade between California and the United States, and this route we are marking will be the artery that makes it possible. After Jed Smith returned with his tales of the rich lands of California, many in our government began to think about ways to use that information to our own benefit."

"And one day, just mebbe we'll reach out and grab the gold ring?" Walters asked. "It's been known to happen in the past, and not just here in the New World. The schoolmaster back home beat a lot of history into his boys when he had the chance."

Beeville's eyes were bright in the firelight. "Just so. I am to watch, to make notes, to draw maps, and to check out the Mexican military presence in Monterey and up and down the coast, if I have the chance. There would be no way to march an army over the country we've covered, but the possibility of an attack from the ocean is something that needs to be explored."

It was, of course, politics as usual, and Malachi understood that. He had conducted his own life and business according to the strict upbringing of his Methodist parents, and he felt that such plotting was not exactly honorable. Still, he was an employee of Beeville, which meant that he also worked for the president himself. It wasn't his place to question the doings of his country's leaders.

"That all?" he asked.

Beeville stared into the fire. His lips barely moved as he said, "Believe me, Malachi, it's quite enough to get us both shot, if word should get out to the wrong ears after we arrive at our destination." Then he rose stiffly and went to his bedroll, where he removed his boots and wrapped himself for sleep.

Damn! Something else to worry about! Malachi thought as he slid, boots and all, into his blankets and rolled over. Though he closed his eyes firmly, the possibilities for trouble contained in this new information kept running through his head until he finally fell asleep from sheer exhaustion.

chapter

— 27 —

Cleve had known fogs all his life. Missouri was no stranger to them, and sometimes in the snowfields of the Rockies the thick mists had settled in and frozen to trees and lodges and people unlucky enough to be out of their shelters.

Here the very air seemed to clog your lungs with moisture. It was hard to see a horse's length ahead as the column of riders moved up into the mountains and the clutter of fern and undergrowth became thicker. Socks whickered, his ears twitching as he tried to pick his way through the tangle that even the string of horses ahead of him had not succeeded in crushing down.

Behind him, Cleve could hear Shadow doing the same. These were horses used to clear, dry air, and this mist was disturbing them.

When the time came to dismount and walk the horses, Cleve dropped back beside his wife and they moved along together, saying little. Yet he knew that she was walking with some of her old spring in her step, and he could feel new energy inside her as he touched her arm with an awkward pat.

He was relieved to find that once she had rid herself of that bad pregnancy, Second Son's strength had returned fully. Still, she seemed somehow sad. The loss was preying on her, he felt, though he could not quite understand how or why, even though Two Big Feet had tried to explain to him the way a woman felt when she lost a child.

He had done his best to keep Second Son distracted, but from time to time he caught an absent look in her dark eyes, and that disturbed him. Perhaps when they reached their goal and beheld the great ocean that neither of them had ever seen, it would cheer her, he thought.

"Did you learn anything more from those Indians back there in the valley?" he asked her. "I liked them, but they seemed mighty scared."

They seemed to be cut off in a tiny pocket of time and space. Even the sounds of those moving ahead and behind were muffled, and voices were blurs, the words indistinguishable. She cocked her head, listened for a moment, and looked up at him. "I learned more than I said, for there is no need to make trouble where none already exists.

"Those people call themselves the Chumash, and they and their ancestors have lived here for more lives of men than there are leaves on the trees. Until the Spanish came, they lived well, for food drops into their hands in this rich country." She listened again for any nearby traveler, but only faint thuds of hooves and hints of voices came to their ears.

"Once the Long Robes built their great lodge there by the bay, the shiny-chested men with terrible weapons began coming inland, searching for people to capture and take back into slavery. They dropped water on the heads of those they caught, and they mumbled words over them. That, they claimed, meant that the bodies of those people belonged to them before they died and their spirits were still slaves after death. *Many* have died, the women told me."

"Of what?" Cleve felt anger rising inside him. He had known too many of his own kind who felt that because these people had a different color and different customs, they were not human. His own mother had felt so, until she came to know his son; even then there were traces of such feeling left, he could tell. Were the Spanish and the Mexicans like that?

"There are sicknesses the Chumash never knew before. Yet worse than the spotted sickness is the hard work, bending in the fields, working among trees grown to bear fruit, when there are already more kinds of fruit here than any sane people might need. Most who die, they say, are worked to death. Even the children.

"Our kind have better sense than to do that. When we

are tired, we stop to rest or to play. But with the Long Robes, the women say, play is forbidden. They must not speak their own tongue or sing their ancient songs. Only the songs in the Prayer Place are allowed, and they are cold and dry and have no heartbeat in them."

"How do they know that? Those in the grove seemed to be free still, in their own place," Cleve said, though he was thinking of the wide eyes and the frightened faces of the small ones lurking behind their mothers.

"Some were taken away but managed to escape. They have told the rest. When there is the risk of being found by white men, they flee and hide in the mountains. We were very lucky to have caught them in the oak grove. There was no cover nearby, and if they had run for the mountains, they knew our horses could catch up with them." Second Son's voice was tense, and as Cleve stared through the mist he saw that her face looked drawn.

He nodded, understanding too well the thing that those people feared. He had talked with Walters, with the Indians, and even with Beeville as they journeyed together; he had listened with attention to their predictions as to the future of the wild lands of the west.

"One day there will be farms in all possible places, towns beside the rivers. White men will own this country," Beeville had told him, gazing across the long reaches of grassland before them.

His words had struck a chill into Cleve's heart. What would be left for the Burning Heart Cheyenne? For his brother-in-law, Singing Wolf, and his son? It would mean the end of the old free life of the plains and the mountains, setting in their places the rigid restrictions he had known in Missouri.

Thinking of that, Cleve felt desolation rise inside him. Where could one go to escape the coming of his kind? First that hidden valley in the Absarokas had been violated by the intrusion of that man Biddle. Now it seemed that all the free country he had loved and longed to live in forever was at risk.

He cleared his throat and spat, tasting gall. "We need to find a place to go," he murmured into Second Son's ear. "Someplace hidden, remote, where my kind can't find it until we're too old to care anymore."

She glanced up questioningly. Cleve struggled to make his meaning clear as they moved forward through a fog that seemed to symbolize their future. "The Plains are already getting crowded with traders and hunters and trappers and even the military. The Rockies are trapped out, hunted out, just about ruined, compared to the way they were when I came west.

"And look at those poor folks back there in the valley—give the Mexicans a few years and they'll have all of them chained to plows, breaking up the land even there, to plant corn and such.

"Seems as if all the white man can do is ruin what he discovers. He finds paradise and he turns it into hell just as fast as he possibly can. I don't want to live like a white man. I left that behind when I was nineteen, and that summer we went back to Missouri taught me that there was no going back to it."

For an instant his wife looked unutterably sad, and he understood why. She, too, had known that the future was going to be hard for them, but it seemed that lacking his insight into his own people, she had not realized just how unhappy it might become.

Before either could speak again, there came a hail from ahead. Two shots, one from a Hawken, one from a trade musket, echoed hollowly through the fog, and Cleve stopped and led his horses aside, out of the way of those behind. Standing beside Second Son, he waited, trying to hear what might be happening.

After a time Quiet Coyote came down the line of people and paused beside the Bennetts. "You see something?" he asked, almost in a whisper. "Something *big*?"

"No." That was Second Son, and her tone was filled with curiosity. "What sort of thing, Coyote?"

He said nothing for a moment, as if trying to find suitable words. Then he pointed to his nose. "Smell bad. *Very* bad. Tall, wide—much big, much stink. But fog so thick we don't see good."

Cleve sniffed, raising his head. Faintly, diluted by fog and a breeze that was just beginning to stir the mist into tendrils, there came to his nostrils an acrid taint, harsher than that of horses or even filthy men. There was something about the smell that made his neck hair want to rise like a wolf's.

"Is that it?" he asked, touching his nose.

Coyote sniffed again. Then he nodded. "Terrible thing, much big, much hairy, but gone in fog. Make no sound."

"A bear," said Second Son. "It must be a big grizzly. But I never smelled one that bad before."

"Mebbe so," said Coyote. "Keep watch. This thing, it very dangerous, I think." Then he was gone down the line, carrying his warning to those behind.

When the column began to move again, the wind was

rising, carrying away the mist before it. Cleve, his mind intent upon watching for this unknown menace, left the conversation unfinished, though he knew that Second Son was already thinking ahead, wondering what refuge they two might find from this world that was pushing them out of their known ways.

chapter

—28—

The strange sadness that had filled her after the child was lost seemed to lighten a bit as Second Son saw the fog begin to wisp away on the wind. With renewed cheerfulness, she remained alert to detect the strange beast that had shown itself to the leaders of the column. Even as she watched and listened for danger, the forest came alive again; more birds and insects than she could ever remember hearing were now calling and fluttering and chirping overhead and underfoot.

Still, she spared a part of her attention to the question

Cleve had posed. For years now she had lived with a white man, though he had grown to become more like her people than his own. But she had spent some part of every summer among his kind, and in that time she felt that she had learned much about their tormented thoughts and their unhappy lives. The short time she had known Cleve's mother had given her some understanding of the terrible things white men taught their children.

No Cheyenne could exist with the lack of honor most white men accepted as normal. No Cheyenne would consent to submit his will to that of another person, as the whites seemed too ready to do. No Cheyenne would waste his energies in piling up possessions that could never be used or enjoyed.

Yet the whites felt that any who did not think as they did were somehow less than men. How could she preserve the heritage of her people for her son—her only child, now? Was there a place in all this wide land that could provide a haven for them and their son, a place in which to work as they willed, to hunt or to rest as they pleased?

She determined, even as she scanned the thick growth on either side of the track, to remember that question. There would be such a spot, she felt, though it might be a long while before they found it.

The column wound up and down successive ridges in the forested mountains, though now the terrain was descending steadily toward some unseen valley beyond the cloaking trees. A whiff of something fresh and strange came to her questing nostrils.

This was no strange animal! No, this was something that one of Smith's men had described to her. . . . Second Son realized what it must be. Inhaling deeply, she felt the salty tang go all through her body, cleaning the cobwebs from her mind and her spirit.

"Yellow Hair!" she called, and he looked around at her. "Smell the wind!"

Smiling, he raised his head and sniffed, as he had done before. But this time his grin widened and his chest expanded. He, too, felt the fresh promise of that clean wind that blew over uncountable miles of water.

She felt her burden of sadness lift even more as she heeled Shadow forward after the riders just ahead. Now those just before her were topping a ridge, and beyond them she could see the sky. The land must drop away sharply beyond, she thought, or else the forest ended. Perhaps their journey was almost done.

Beside Cleve, with Socks and Shadow nickering in answer to the excited whinnies of the other horses, she rode out of the trees and halted on the stony brow of a ridge overlooking a long panorama.

Downslope, there was a pattern of fields, some gold, some tan; some patches were brown, where the land had been broken like that she had seen in Missouri. Blocks of small growth were dropped among the fields, and she knew those must be the fruit trees or the vines the Chumash had mentioned.

Even from such a distance, she thought she could spot toiling figures there. Were they picking the fruits of the orchards, so late in the year? But she knew nothing of such things, and she looked beyond, toward the huddle of lodges.

Earth-toned buildings, shaped differently from those she had seen in Missouri, centered a cluster of huts. Big trees leaned over them, she thought, though the entire scene was very small with distance.

Cleve touched her shoulder and pointed. She raised her eyes a bit and saw the long blue line that she had thought was sky. But it was no sky at all; it was an endless expanse of water that reflected blue from the cloudless vault above.

"The Great Water!" she murmured. "I am looking upon that now, and it is more—much more—than I guessed it would be."

Cleve, too, was staring, his eyes, almost the color of the sky and the sea, wide and bright. "By damn, I never thought I'd live to see it, but there it is, big as life. And bigger." He grinned down at her.

Second Son felt a great smile growing inside her as well. As the riders started down the long slope toward the bay, in whose curve the small settlement lay like a cluster of flowers, she knew that this was the end of their journey.

They had come to California at last!

Author's Note

There was, in fact, an actual expedition like the one I described in this book. It was organized by Joseph Walker, a remarkable man and a fine planner and organizer. At the bidding of Benjamin Bonneville, he announced, at the Green River Rendezvous of 1833, his plan to find an easier route to California than the one tried by Jedediah Smith some years earlier.

Instead of taking the southern route, which went around the easier end of the Sierras, but by so doing crossed the worst of the desert country, Walker chose to go north of

Salt Lake, angling across Nevada to catch the Humboldt River and follow it up toward the Sierras. Because of his foresight in supplying many extra horses and a great deal of dried meat, secured before beginning the main journey, his people came through in much better condition than Smith's earlier party.

That actual expedition formed the framework of this fictional one. Instead of being a huge man like Walker, my Malachi Walters is a small wiry one, though he shares the planning and leadership abilities of the original.

Incidents along the way resemble those that actually occurred on the Walker trip. The Diggers (Paiutes), unused to seeing anyone with so many possessions, stalked their route and circled their camps. They actually asked, when trying to find a way to take what the whites owned, to come in and talk with Walker and his leaders. Walker, too, refused that request. Although this episode resembles an event recorded by Walker, I have created my own sequence of events leading to the final confrontation with the Paiutes.

Similarly, the entire story of crossing the Sierras is fictional, but is based on true accounts of such crossings, including that of the Donner party.

Although it was rumored for years that Benjamin Bonneville was an agent of the U.S. government, I have been unable to substantiate this claim. However, I have allowed Ben Beeville to do so—complete with official documents from the president to the officials at Monterey, although the story ends before he presents those to the governor at the Presidio.

The brief mention of the enslavement of the Chumash by the Spanish is accurate. This was the method used by the missionaries, who managed to enslave and convert numbers of those peaceful coastal people. By the end of the mission era, they also managed to kill seventy-five percent of their converts through disease and overwork.

The animal that Quiet Coyote saw in the mist as the party crossed the last mountain range was, of course, the Sasquatch. Although there has been much nay-saying in modern times, a long tradition asserts its existence among the coastal tribes, before the white man arrived. Indians had no earthly reason to create a hoax, and they were certainly not liars of our caliber.

This story is not history. Too often, readers of historical fiction become confused about fact and fiction. I like to make that difference very clear. I *have* used historical fact, but I have mixed it well with invented characters and incidents.

However, this was a fascinating era, and many historical works and journal articles can be found in libraries if the reader wants to glimpse how things really were in those wild and far-off times.

If you enjoyed PASSAGE WEST by John Killdeer, be sure to look for the next novel in his MOUNTAIN MAJESTY series:

THE FAR HORIZON

Mountain Man Cleve Bennett and his Cheyenne wife Second Son, in the company of the Malachi Walters expedition, have survived the treacherous journey over the Rocky Mountains and into California. Arriving in Monterey, they are welcomed by the Mexican governor, but the local priest becomes obsessed with subjugating Cleve's "heathen" wife. As Cleve and Second Son continue north toward the Columbia River they discover that the evil padre has sent a band of thugs in pursuit. But his crusade is no longer merely for Second Son's soul. He wants a share of Cleve Bennett's unintentional discovery: gold.

Look for Mountain Majesty Book 6: THE FAR HORIZON, on sale in Summer 1994, wherever Bantam Books are sold.